PENGUIN BOOKS

PIG

Andrew Cowan was born in Corby and educated at Beanfield Comprehensive and the University of East Anglia. He lives in Norwich with the writer Lynne Bryan and their daughter Rose. Before winning a Betty Trask Award for *Pig* in 1993, he worked as a postman, an oral historian, a cleaner in a cake factory and a chartered librarian. His second novel, *Common Ground*, was written with the assistance of a Scottish Arts Council Bursary and will be published by Michael Joseph in 1996.

Pig also won the Ruth Hadden Memorial Prize, the Author's Club First Novel Award, the *Sunday Times* Young Writer of the Year Award and a Scottish Arts Council Book Award, and it was shortlisted for the John Steinbeck Award.

D1490493

ANDREW COWAN

PIG

PENGUIN BOOKS

PENGUIN BOOKS

Published by the Penguin Group
Penguin Books Ltd, 27 Wrights Lane, London W8 5TZ, England
Penguin Books USA Inc., 375 Hudson Street, New York, New York 10014, USA
Penguin Books Australia Ltd, Ringwood, Victoria, Australia
Penguin Books Canada Ltd, 10 Alcorn Avenue, Toronto, Ontario, Canada M4V 3B2
Penguin Books (NZ) Ltd, 182–190 Wairau Road, Auckland 10, New Zealand

Penguin Books Ltd, Registered Offices: Harmondsworth, Middlesex, England

First published by Michael Joseph 1994
Published in Penguin Books 1995
3 5 7 9 10 8 6 4 2

Copyright © Andrew Cowan, 1994
All rights reserved

The moral right of the author has been asserted

Printed in England by Clays Ltd, St Ives plc

Except in the United States of America, this book is sold subject
to the condition that it shall not, by way of trade or otherwise, be lent,
re-sold, hired out, or otherwise circulated without the publisher's
prior consent in any form of binding or cover other than that in
which it is published and without a similar condition including this
condition being imposed on the subsequent purchaser

For David,
to the memory of
Dobbie

Author's note: I have a Mum and Dad, and a brother.
They do not appear in this novel.

ACKNOWLEDGEMENTS

I would like to thank the Association for Scottish Literary Studies, who published the first chapter of this novel in their anthology *Pig Squealing* (*New Writing Scotland 10*); Tony Drane, who pointed me in this direction; Robert Hamberger, who prompted the story; Ged Lawson, who gave me the pig; Alastair Whitson and Tim Preston, who read the manuscript; but especially Lynne Bryan, for everything.

ONE

IT WAS the pig that woke my grandfather on the morning Gran died. It was squealing outside in the garden.
The noise didn't wake him at once but crept into his sleep
and brought on a dream. He dreamt he was back home in
Glasgow, in the slaughterhouse where he first worked
beside Gran. They were children then, barely into their
teens, but in his dream they were already old, shrunken and
wrinkled, twice the age of their parents. Grandad was
trying to butcher a pig. He struck it repeatedly on the back
of its skull with a mawl, but the animal was stubborn and
refused to buckle beneath him. All the while it was squealing
Gran was squatting by a tub of scalding hot water, ready to
scrape it, quietly waiting. In the shadows behind her their
parents were huddled together and whispering. Grandad
began to pour sweat as freely as the blood which flowed

from the pig, until he could hardly see what he was doing. 'There's nae strength in me, Agnes,' he said. But Gran didn't respond. She dipped her elbow in the water and smiled to the parents, who cooed and muttered admiringly. He continued to strike at the pig, crying now in frustration, still sweating, and when he woke his vest and pyjamas were soaking.

The room was sunk in near darkness, the curtains drawn tightly. He tried to gauge the time by the sunlight showing under the door, but he knew it was late. The pig did not normally squeal unless it was hungry. He didn't realize at first about Gran. 'The beast's after her grub, Agnes,' he said. But of course she didn't reply.

It was unlike her not to wake first. Before my grandfather retired he used to start work at six every morning, but he never rose unless he was called. Whilst he slept on, Gran would climb from their bed and draw back the curtains. She stepped into her slippers and went down to the kitchen, already fastening her raincoat. As the kettle started to warm she would light her first cigarette and sit down by the stove. She tapped the ash into the palm of her hand, staring out through the window at the lights fading over the steel-works, the sun coming up behind them. And when her cigarette was finished and the water was ready she would tip her ash in the sink and fill a large teapot, then go out to the garden with a bucket of scraps for the pig. Much later she returned to coax Grandad awake with a cup of stewed tea.

Her routine did not alter when Grandad stopped working, nor when his leg was removed a few years after that. It was amputated just below the left knee and he was given a plastic replacement. The hospital provided a walking frame too, but his wound never properly healed and he was unable to stand for more than an hour each day. The false leg and frame soon became part of the furniture, dusted over as regularly as the sideboard and ornaments. I was born a few months after he had his operation, and in a different hospital, but Grandad always insisted I arrived on the same day in the ward next to his. He said the swap was a fair one.

Shortly after he came back to the house from the hospital Gran had their bed carried downstairs to the front room. She allowed him to sleep for an extra hour each morning but she continued to rise at just the same time. She was a small round woman and constantly busy. The pattern of her days was firmly established. It was the regularity of her daily existence which made me prefer their house to my own and when I was younger I often pleaded to be allowed to stay overnight. I slept on a lumpy mattress upstairs in the back bedroom, a part of the house they had almost abandoned. Their old bedroom remained empty, facing out to the front garden.

Grandad accepted losing his limb quite cheerfully, but neither of my grandparents would give up their cigarettes. It was the smoking, the surgeon had told them, that was responsible for his leg turning bad. Grandad would light a cigarette the moment he woke, and he lit one too as he lay listening to the pig squealing that morning. It made him cough, but it helped bring him round from his dream.

When his coughing finally subsided he turned over to touch Gran. 'D'ye no hear the animal squawking, Agnes?' he said, and felt around in the space where she ought to have been. The sheets were cool and unruffled. He pushed himself upright and saw her at once. She was sitting in her nightdress by the sideboard, in the chair where she would rest each evening to remove her stockings and shoes. Her arms hung stiffly at her sides. Even in the darkness there could be no doubt what was wrong, but he continued to talk to her. 'What's up, Agnes?' he said, and stubbed out the cigarette. 'Is the motor no running this morning?'

He heaved himself from the bed slowly, feeling the damp in his clothes, the cold on his chest. His good leg creaked under his weight and he had to gasp for his breath. He paused after the effort, holding onto the arms of his wheel-chair, all the time watching Gran. When his breathing had steadied he twisted his body into the seat and lifted the brakes, rolled himself to the curtains. In the daylight he could see her more clearly. She might have been asleep the way she was seated. He approached warily, and whispered her name. 'What's up?' he asked her. Her mouth hung slightly open as if about to reply. She seemed to be returning his gaze, her eyelids partially closed, patiently watching him. He touched her chin with his thumb and shivered at the touch. 'It's nae wonder you're cold, Agnes,' he said. Her nightdress lay open, displaying her ribcage. In places the skin was as white as the cloth, but elsewhere there were blotches, like someone who had spent too long by a fire. He drew the neck of her nightdress together, fastened the buttons, then he dragged a blanket from the bed and draped her beneath it.

There was no telephone in their house because Gran wouldn't have one, she didn't like them. The clock on the sideboard showed five to eight, an hour after the milkman usually called. It was half a mile to their nearest neighbour, a mile and a half to the edge of the town. Grandad decided to wait for the newsboy. He dressed himself with fumbling hands and fished in his pocket for loose change. He would ask the boy when he came to cycle to a call box and dial 999; he would offer the coins for his trouble. Grandad always had money. Whenever I called he would give me a handful, quietly, almost secretively, whilst Gran was in the kitchen brewing tea. And later, when I got up to leave,

Gran would follow me to the back door with her purse, just in case he'd forgotten. 'Did he give you your wages, son?' she would ask me. They always called it my wages and they wouldn't let me refuse.

Their bedroom downstairs had once been the front parlour, with a door that opened onto the garden, now seldom used, the lock too stiff for Grandad to open. He turned and wheeled through the smaller back room and the conservatory, into the kitchen and out to the yard, around the side of the house. The air was thick and warm and he felt the first drops of rain on his arms. At the top of the garden the pig pushed her snout over the rim of her pen and watched him approaching. She sniffed at the air and pricked up her ears, snorted and squealed excitedly. As he drew near he offered his palm and spoke to her softly. 'Empty-handed, pet,' he said. The pig butted his fingers and dropped out of sight, snuffling around the floor of her sty. Grandad stared along the rough track that led to the main road. He tapped the coins on the wheel of his chair. In the distance he could hear the first rush of traffic along the dual carriageway, an ambulance receding towards the estates of the new town.

TWO

ONE AFTERNOON, three years before Gran died, I came home from school to find my parents wrestling on the staircase. I was twelve years old. My father had been drinking and the house smelled of beer. He was slumped on top of my mother a few steps beneath the top landing, struggling to pin down her arms. His trousers were slipping and I noticed a rash across the small of his back. Mum was wearing only her dressing gown and her hair was unpinned, grey and dishevelled. I remembered she was unwell and had taken the day off from work. As she shifted beneath him her dressing gown fell open.

I did not try to separate them, but watched in silence from the foot of the stairs. They were remote and unconnected with me, two strangers, and I thought about walking away, perhaps to visit my sister. But I was unable to move.

I leant my head on the wall. Some children were shouting in the square at the front of our house. They were chasing a football, their footsteps resounding over the concrete, echoing from the buildings around us. I knew who they were from their voices and I imagined myself playing with them, my mother indoors in the kitchen, Dad returning from work. Then their ball rattled our window and for a moment everything was quiet.

I lifted my head and saw that my mother was crying. She was no longer struggling and her face was turned towards mine. I became conscious of her voice saying my name, quietly at first, and then louder, until she was sobbing. Dad loosened his grip on her wrists and pushed himself upright. His neck and temples were red, glistening with sweat, and as he tried to focus his eyes I reached for the door. His voice pursued me as I ran from the house. I could hear it still as I walked along the side of the dual carriageway to my grandparents' house.

Gran did not seem surprised to see me. When I appeared at the top of her garden she was digging the allotment, wearing a cloth cap that had once belonged to my grandfather. Her wellington boots were muddy and turned down at the top, exposing the veins on her legs. As she stood her fork in the soil she called for me to go inside, then started to follow. Grandad was sitting in his armchair in the back room. He looked up with widening eyes and held out his hand. Two plumes of smoke curled from his nose. His palm was moist and warm. 'Sit yourself down, son,' he said. 'Just in time for the news.' He did not ask why I had come, and neither of them mentioned my parents, though several times Gran looked at me closely. Later in the evening, when the television was on, she made some sandwiches and stood over my shoulder whilst I ate them. We listened to Grandad as he described the afternoon's horse racing, the names of the jockeys and favourites. Then I helped prepare some food for the pig.

I returned each afternoon that week, taking a route from school that avoided my home, out to the edge of the town and along a road bordered by hedges and yellowing trees. Gran made sure I was fed and found things for me to do until it began to grow dark, by which time I knew my father would have gone to his pub. I walked home slowly and lingered outside our back door before I went in, counting to a hundred. The house was usually in darkness, my mother in bed. She still wasn't going to work. My brother was away in the army.

When I arrived at my grandparents' house on the Friday I found Dad's car parked at the top of the rise. For a moment I hesitated, and approached the cottage warily, half-expecting he would appear from the side of the house, wanting to know why I wasn't at home. I avoided his eyes as I came through the door. He was sitting beside Mum in the back room, hunched forwards and nodding his head. Gran was telling him something but stopped when she saw me. I sat on the edge of the sofa beside Mum and she placed her hand on my knee. She smiled thinly, began to tell Gran a story about someone she had met in the doctor's reception. Dad held a cigarette between his forefinger and thumb, but didn't smoke it. Occasionally he tapped some ash in a saucer by his feet and coughed quietly. He rubbed at his eyes. Like my mother he looked very tired. I wondered when they would say something to me, but no one asked any questions about school and no mention was made of my absence at tea-times.

Finally my grandfather said, 'Did you see the pig on your way in, son?' He had not spoken until then and his voice was almost a whisper. I shook my head. The others had stopped talking and I sensed they were waiting for something. The clock on the mantelpiece struck half past five. 'Come on then,' he said, 'We'll go take a wee look.' I kicked the brakes from his wheelchair and pushed it towards him. He gripped the armrests to steady himself before standing.

Seagulls circled above us. When the steelworks had closed the previous year a tip had been started near the far edge of Gran's garden, where the land fell away to a railway cutting. The quarries and earth piles beyond were fenced off and newly signposted, owned now by a leisure company. I took a deep breath and stepped onto the lawn. The air was cool and smelled of damp soil. I was glad we'd come out of the house. Grandad lit a fresh cigarette and nodded towards Dad's car. 'Not often we see that up here these days.'

'No,' I said. 'It looks strange.'

'Aye, son,' he said. 'So it does.' He flicked his match to the lawn and drew in some smoke, then he said, 'They've a few things to get off their chests, Danny. Your mum and dad.' I gave a small nod and faced away to the quarries. 'We'd best leave them to it, eh? Let your gran sort it.'

In the distance a group of men were walking by a ridge of blue earth, carrying shovels. I watched them descend out of sight, and then asked, 'Why did you want to look at the pig?'

'She's pregnant!' he said. 'Did your gran no tell ye?'

'No.'

'The farmer's boy fetched her this morning.' He loosened the brakes on his chair. 'Brought her back before dinner-time. Come on, we'll see how she's doing.'

The pig lay on her belly in the angle of two walls, eying us calmly. Her home was an Anderson shelter, packed inside with bales of straw, facing out to a long concrete run. An apple tree gave shade from the sunshine in summer, dropped fruit into her sty in the autumn. On one side of the pen was a dry stone wall which stretched the length of the garden. The other three sides were breezeblock, built behind the railway sleepers that still remained of the original walls. A deflated football hung down from a chain in one corner. Two sheets of corrugated plastic sheltered her feeding trough and the old sink she drank from, both of them cemented to the ground. She lay quite still, her ears pricked as Grandad talked about the other pigs they had kept and the best way of breeding them, how it used to be in the old days. He liked to tell stories. As he spoke he leaned forwards, moving his hands in the air to describe things, his face constantly changing. I listened to every word, but my eyes watched the house, expecting my parents. He explained about boars and how they were made into hogs. 'Because they're awfy bad-tempered beasts,' he said. 'It's nae wonder they get castrated. Your gran would never keep one, no for breeding anyway. And at one time ye couldnae sell the meat off a boar either, because folk objected to the smell. It was like piss, awfy pissy smell.' He made a sour expression and tossed away the stub of his cigarette. 'We used tae castrate them ourselves, Danny. Your gran and I. She had the steadier hand so it was my job tae hold them, keep the wee buggers docile. Dab of spirit beforehand, ye know, disinfectant. Then your gran would pinch up the first ball, make a wee cut, and squeeze it out. She cut the cords very carefully because ye didnae want blood everywhere, no in the kitchen. Because we had to do it in the kitchen d'ye see, son, away from the mother. Then your gran would take the balls to Mrs McIntyre down the road there, in a wee bowl. She fed them tae her dogs. Her man was a Scot too, and a fixer. He helped me put up this sty – he told me he came by the sleepers at the Corporation, in the yards. But he came by every bloody thing at the Corporation!' Grandad laughed, wiped some spittle from his lips with the back of his hand. 'Died of cancer in the end,' he said.

When my mother and father finally emerged from the house it had begun to turn cold. The sky was darkening overhead and they were wearing their coats. Gran followed behind with a blanket. She draped it over my grandfather's legs and wheeled him back to the house, stopping briefly to wave when Dad started the car. He drove home in silence and my mother stared out of the window. But they did not seem angry, just thoughtful. I pressed my face to the glass and watched the cars shoot by in the other direction. 'The pig's up the spout again,' I told them.

The following weekend my grandmother asked me, 'Is your father still using his pub, Danny?' She was sitting by the fireplace with her knitting, and didn't look up. Grandad and I were watching a football match, Manchester United and Leeds.

'Not this week,' I said.

She paused and counted some stitches, whispering under her breath. A little while after she said, 'He'll be doing some gardening then?'

I thought for a moment. 'He's says he's making a patio,' I told her.

'And is he?'

'I suppose so,' I said.

'A patio, Joe,' she said to my grandfather.

Grandad looked at her seriously, and then started to laugh. He turned his face to the television. 'Dinnae put the flags out yet,' he said.

THREE

ALTHOUGH MY father stopped drinking that summer, and stayed at home most evenings, he made slow progress on his patio. Three months and three weeks after he bought the cement the pig gave birth to a litter of five, the last that Gran would allow her. The piglets were tiny and sickly and none of them lived to be sold. The pig herself became poorly, lay quietly on her bedding for days, hardly eating or drinking. We did not expect her to live, but Gran spent hours calmly waiting, offering food and mixing up medicines, until finally the animal came round. In other years my grandmother had replaced the sows before they were old, and most were reared solely for eating, but this one she decided to keep as her last. She said she wanted the dung for her garden. My grandfather seemed pleased and teased her she was turning soft, but Gran had refused to admit it. She never spoke to the pig kindly or quietly again, and always grumbled about the work that it caused her.

Whilst the pig was still farrowing, and the patio half-laid, my father got a job on the night shift of a cosmetics factory. Mum was employed there during the day, packing toiletries into boxes for supermarkets. Dad sat alone in a room reading magazines. He was a security guard. It was the first time he had worked since the steelworks had made him redundant, and although he was given a uniform – a green cap and a jacket – he had to supply his own trousers. Each evening before leaving he sat in our kitchen and polished his shoes, listening to the radio, a cigarette burning on the edge of the worktop beside him. He slept through most of the day, and he said he had no time for the garden. For three years the patio remained half-finished. A full sack of cement was propped up outside the back door, two piles of paving slabs sat alongside the dustbin. Gradually we learnt to ignore them; neither of my parents were gardeners, and they only used the back door for the bins or the clothes line.

When the policewoman brought the news about Gran my father had just gone to bed from his shift. It was my brother Richard who answered the door. He was dressed in only his underpants and his face was pale and unshaven. He waved for me to sit down. He was holding a beer can, a cigarette between two fingers. I supposed he was expecting a friend – they often called in the mornings, and stopped by only briefly, never coming inside – but I did not expect the voice on the doorstep to be female. Although sometimes my brother would tell me about the women he knew, he did not give them names and they were never invited to come to our house. As he led the policewoman into the living room I felt a moment of relief that she wasn't a girlfriend, and said 'Hello,' waiting to hear what she would tell him. But she pulled off her cap and stood with her back to the window, not speaking, clearly waiting for Richard. It was raining outside and her uniform was damp. As I looked to my brother he narrowed an eye and peered into his can before drinking. 'You'd better go and wake Dad,' he told. me. 'Your grannie's kicked the bucket.'

He did not come with us in the car to fetch Mum, and my father drove very carefully, as he always did. At the junction to the main road he glanced in his mirror and said, 'Seems a bit early for Richard to be drinking.' I shrugged my shoulders. 'Not really,' I said. We passed some people standing at a bus shelter, an old man posting a letter. Two boys from my school emerged from a side street, walking quickly and laughing. They were called Spider and Stan and their names were sprayed all around the estate. As I turned to watch them Dad switched on the radio and we caught the end of a weather report. The weatherman sounded cheerful. Dad turned the sound low, and said, 'He's putting on a lot of weight anyway.'

Ten minutes later we arrived at the gates of the industrial estate. A guard waved from inside a brick hut and my father tooted his horn, accelerated down the wide driveway. There were no other people in sight, just cars and lorries and white factory buildings, a few flags on their roofs. My grandmother had died, but nothing was different from usual. In the car park Dad turned off the engine and lit up a cigarette. 'Won't be long,' he said. 'Let your mum have the front seat.'

I watched as he walked away. His head was bowed against the rain and the bottoms of his trousers were flapping. He didn't seem to be in any hurry and it was a while before he reappeared. Mum came out before him, holding a white bonnet to her head. She was still dressed in her factory apron, white pumps on her feet, and as she drew closer I tried to make out if she looked worried or upset, but her face was obscured by the rain. When she climbed into the car she pulled off her bonnet and quickly examined herself in the mirror, then she took one of Dad's cigarettes. She turned to face me, pressing her mouth to a smile, and I saw that her fingers were trembling.

'Grandad found her,' I said.

She looked to my father and asked, 'Did they say what it was?'

'A stroke.'

Mum made a sighing noise. She gazed up at the clouds. 'Raining as well,' she said.

'Soon pass,' said my father. And he turned the keys in his ignition.

Before we reached my grandparents' house Mum finished one cigarette and started another. She stubbed out the second as we turned onto the track that led up to the cottage. An ambulance was moving off, coming towards us, and Dad reversed back to the main road to allow it to pass, lifting his thumb to the driver. He kept one hand on his gearstick and advanced smoothly when the ambulance had gone by. Mum bowed her head, took a sudden deep breath, fixing her eyes on the windscreen. 'Okay?' said my father, and she nodded. I watched the ambulance departing and tried to imagine my grandmother inside it. But the woman I pictured could have been anybody and I looked instead to the house, the empty allotment, a police car parked at the top of the rise. As we pulled up to the gate Dad nodded at the police car and said, 'Best behaviour now, Danny.' He winked as he opened his door.

Outside the pig was circling in her sty. She jumped at the wall when she saw us and Dad made a clucking noise with his tongue, pausing to scratch at the back of her ear. I stopped to watch him, my hands in my pockets. I wanted to tell him something about her, something Gran might have said, but I couldn't think of anything he wouldn't already know. Mum called to us from the side of the house and we followed her round. She waited by the back door, and rapped twice on the wood as she ushered us through. 'There's no need to knock,' I told her.

Although they had several kinds of heater, electric and paraffin, my grandparents still kept a coal fire in their back room. They sat in armchairs on either side of the mantelpiece, Grandad's wheelchair sometimes empty between them. A small sofa was pushed back against the longest wall and the television stood on a trolley beside it. As we entered the room the first person I saw was the policeman, rising stiffly from my grandmother's armchair. Grandad looked round with a dazzled expression, as though for a moment unsure who we were. Then he said hoarsely, 'Come in. Agnes is no long away.' His hair was standing on end, grey stubble covered the roll of his chin. When Mum sat down on the edge of the sofa the policeman indicated for my father to follow him outside, but Dad said, 'I think it's the wife you want,' and stood to one side. He looked at Mum and said, 'Jean?'

I went to Gran's chair, facing Grandad, but it seemed larger than usual, less comfortable, and I moved instead to the wheelchair. The room was smoke-filled and dark, and whilst Mum was outside in the conservatory we sat without speaking. I listened to the rain on the window. Grandad rubbed his hands slowly, one over the other, gazing down at the fireplace. The hearth was cold and brushed clean and the fire wouldn't be lit until the summer was over.

When Mum returned alone to the room my father took out his cigarettes and nudged her to take one, pointing with the packet at Grandad. She sat on the arm of my grandfather's chair and rested one hand on his shoulder. 'Dad?' she said softly, and offered the cigarette. Her tone was unsure and he looked at her vaguely. Then his chest heaved and I saw he was crying.

Afterwards I fetched his whisky from the bedroom and we waited to hear what had happened. Grandad held his glass to his chest and continued to gaze at the fireplace. Mum's hand rubbed at his shoulder. She was sitting close by him, looking down at the floor. Their faces were in shadow. Rain drummed on the roof of the conservatory and from the top of the garden I could hear the pig squealing.

Finally I said, 'Did the pig get her breakfast today, Grandad?'

He raised his eyes to look at me. 'What was that, son?'

'Has the pig been fed yet?'

'The pig?' He was frowning. 'Can ye hear her still?'

'Outside,' I said.

'Aye, son. Aye.' He nodded, and slowly he brought his glass to his lips. 'She woke me this morning ye know, squawking and squealing. She hasnae had a bite since yesterday teatime. Your gran fed her something, the back of six o'clock.' Mum shifted uneasily on the arm of his chair, and Grandad said, 'Because they've bellies like ours ye know, son. They like their grub.'

'I know,' I said.

My father sipped at his whisky and leaned forwards. He rolled the glass in his palms. 'She'll be some age now, Joe, the pig?'

Grandad knitted his brows. 'She'll be for the slaughter-house anyway,' he said. 'I cannae mind her. No now. I cannae look after myself.'

'You'll be alright,' Mum said, and she rose to empty his

ashtray in the fireplace. She switched on the main light and refilled his glass, then looked around for Dad's cigarettes.

I said, 'What if I looked after her, Grandad?'

'Aye, son,' he said. 'You can see to her. There's a coat in the kitchen there, on the back of the door, keep the rain off.'

'All the time, I mean.'

Grandad nodded again, but he didn't appear to have heard me. As he sipped at his drink his eyes lost their focus, and my father said quietly, 'It's a lot to take on, Danny.'

'Too much,' said my mother, and struck a match to her cigarette.

FOUR

DESPITE THE pig, it was quiet where my grandparents lived. Their house faced out to fields and quarries, the new estates of the town in the distance. Where the steelworks had once stood at the rear of the house, now there was nothing, a vast open space littered with rubble and rusting machine parts. Theirs had been the last in a terrace of similar cottages which stretched down as far as the main road. Each house had its own name, carved on a plaque just over the door. My grandparents' cottage was called Kelvin, which was a river in Glasgow, close to where they lived before they came down to England. It stood alone now, shored up on one side by a scaffold of timber. The others were demolished when the people died or moved out, their long gardens overtaken by nettles.

My grandmother's garden was four times as wide as the

neighbouring plots and divided in two by a pathway. She kept a lawn and some flowering shrubs in front of the house – rosebushes mostly; a japonica, magnolia, and several others I didn't know the names of. At the side of the house was her allotment, where sometimes she allowed me to dig over the soil or help spread manure from the pig pen. She was proud of the vegetables she grew and thought hard about what to plant where. The best specimens I usually carried home to my mother, wrapped up in newspaper. Most of the rest went back as feed for the pig.

The garden now was thick with green, and the rain had eased to a drizzle. In the farthest corner of the allotment two apple trees were beginning to fruit. Carrots and turnips and onions showed clearly through the damp soil. As I came around the side of the building I rattled the swill bucket and saw the pig's face appear above the sty wall, twitching and silent. I was wearing my grandmother's rain-coat and wellingtons, and when I copied her call the pig swung out of sight. A thread of saliva trailed behind her. She was grunting wildly when I reached her.

With a heave I balanced the pail on the rim of one wall and tilted it carefully. It was heavy and awkward to pour and much of the swill spattered onto the ground at the side of the trough. The pig began gorging before the last of the mixture had fallen. In minutes her trough had been emp-tied. She cleaned up around it, snuffling and burping, then drank from a puddle and returned to her shelter. I stared across to the quarries. Far away in the distance I could see the Enterprise Zone, a cluster of tiny white factories and conifer trees. It looked like a planner's scale model and I couldn't imagine that people would work there. Not long after the construction began I had pointed it out to my grandmother. She was thinning some leeks and as she rose from her knees she placed a hand on the small of her back.

She peered in the direction of my finger, then shook her head angrily. 'Can't see them,' she said. 'Too far away.'

At about the same time a hoarding appeared on the far side of the railway cutting, facing across to Gran's garden. It stood at the head of the tip and said *LeisureLand* in large cheerful letters. Helicopters and rockets arched over the words. Beneath them was a line of children and adults about to enter a dome. Similar signs faced out onto every road that skirted the old site of the steelworks, and sometimes in the evening paper there were letters asking when the work was supposed to begin. One was headlined 'Fantasy Land?' I preferred to read the company's replies, which were more optimistic.

The same company also owned the land on which my grandparents had their cottage. One Saturday, a year after the steelworks had closed, Gran had showed me an envelope. It might have been good or bad news for she made no comment and her expression was neutral. As I read the contents aloud she went quietly from the room and Grandad shook his head sadly. 'She's a wee bit cut up about it, son,' he said, though I couldn't understand why. The company had acquired the cottage when they bought the rights to the steel site. Their address was in Holland, and they apologized for any inconvenience caused by the scheduled construction. Afterwards I went outside to help in the garden, and Gran looked cross when I mentioned the letter. We were standing at either end of a frame of broad beans, tossing pods into a basket that sat half-way between us. No more words were spoken and when the basket was full she slipped her arm through mine and we walked back to the house.

I looked across to where this year's crop was growing. The trellis she had built was almost obscured behind a thin bush of foliage and soon the pods would start forming again. Fleetingly I saw her as she stretched to reach the topmost of the leaves, and realized then that I was going to cry. Staring hard at the bush I repeated the word *dead* softly aloud until it caught in my throat. I felt my mouth tighten, tears filling my eyes, and I crouched with my back to the wall of the sty. I hid myself from the house, took deep breaths that turned into sobs, heard the pig becoming restless behind me.

When finally I made myself stand the pig was looking over the wall. I blinked hard and glanced to the house, quickly wiped my nose on the sleeve of Gran's raincoat. Although the drizzle continued to fall the sun was showing over the quarries. Walking slowly, my hands in the pockets of the raincoat, I set off through the allotment. I saw spaces where I would need to plant for autumn and winter, vegetable rows that were ready for thinning, weeds starting to sprout. The brussels were already beginning to topple. I crouched and packed the soil tight round the base of a stem, then shuffled along to the next. The rain came heavily again, stopped before I completed the row.

As I stood to wipe the damp soil from my knees I saw a red transit approaching from the main road. It bumped noisily over the ruts in the track and braked a few feet behind Dad's car. The two men who climbed out were both dressed in blue overalls, the driver stocky and bearded, his partner younger and taller, tattooed on both forearms. A radio crackled inside the cab. Without looking at me they went to the rear of the van and bent from sight, then the driver emerged with a television set. He puffed out his cheeks and adjusted his grip, began walking to the top of the slope, to where the tip was. The other man followed. He carried a black bin bag in either hand. His hair was long and greasy, tied back in a pony tail. He was about the same age as my brother and I thought that I recognized him.

I went across to the sty and stood by the swill bucket, watching as the men returned to the van. They made another four trips to the tip, and each time the driver carried some piece of furniture, his partner a couple of bin bags. They didn't vary their pace and when their work was complete the driver got into the van and immediately started the engine. The younger man went to close the rear doors but didn't climb into the cab. As he strolled towards me he unwrapped a chewing gum and stood where he could see into the sty. I took a step nearer the gate. 'Is the pig yours?' he said.

'Yes.'

He tossed the wrapping paper to one side. 'She'll take some looking after.'

'Not especially,' I said. The back door of the cottage opened and slammed shut. I heard my father cough as he came around the side of the house. 'The real work's in the garden,' I said.

The man nodded, gazed down at the pig. His nose was long and sharp and his face very white. On his left arm there was a picture of a tombstone, a bulging heart and a dagger. The tattoo was familiar. He was a friend of my brother's; he had been to our house. As Dad's footsteps came closer behind me the man looked up and said, 'Alright Bill?'

'Not bad,' my father replied. 'You?'

The man tugged on the end of his nose, cocked a thumb at the sty. 'Just admiring the livestock.'

'I didn't think you were in that game, Craig.'

Craig made a vague gesture with his hand. He smiled, showing his gums. They were red, as if he'd been eating. In the van behind him his partner was reading a paper, the engine still running. 'Now and again,' he said. 'I've an uncle works out at the abattoir.'

'So what do you reckon?' asked Dad.

'Sausages,' said Craig. 'Meat pies maybe.'

My father laughed, and I told them, 'She's not for sale anyway.'

Craig smiled again. He looked at my father. 'Richard's brother?'

'That's it.' Dad placed his hand on my shoulder. 'This is the brains of the family.' He tried to ruffle my hair but I pulled away from him, picked up the bucket. Craig smiled, glanced quickly over his shoulder. I saw the chewing gum balled on his tongue. He spat it out as he turned to the van. 'Tell Richard I'll see him Friday,' he said.

We watched the van reverse to the main road, Craig immobile in the passenger seat, then my father said, 'Come on,' and I followed him back to the house. As we came to the door he hesitated. 'Grandad's not taken it too well, Danny,' he said. 'He depended a lot on your gran.'

'I know,' I said.

'We'll have to think how he's going to manage now. On his own.'

I felt the damp on my neck and shivered. I hunched up my shoulders. 'The bungalow next door to us is empty,' I said. 'He could move in there.'

My father nodded doubtfully, pushed open the door. In a quieter voice he said, 'It's probably not that simple, Danny.'

'You mean you think he should be put in a home.'

As we stepped into the kitchen he said, 'Some of these places are very well kept, son.'

FIVE

THE PEBBLE flew in a curve from my arm and struck the highest branches of an oak tree. A cluster of birds scattered noisily and black against the clear sky. I watched as they disappeared, felt the warmth of the sun through my jacket. It was the hottest day of the summer so far and clouds of small flies hung in the air. An ice cream van tinkled close by and from somewhere far off came the sound of people cheering, perhaps a sports meeting, the end of a race. The idea made me feel weary. I loosened my tie and bent to pick another stone from the flower bed. Beyond the crematorium gardens there was a workman on a motorized lawnmower. He wore a white floppy hat, but no shirt, and he was steering the machine with one hand. A Union Jack billowed gently on the roof of the factory behind him. I waited until he turned from the trees and then I took a few paces into the sun, aiming again for the birds. The stone bounced twice and skidded into the factory wall. The workman switched off his engine, lifted a hand to his eyes. I stepped back into the shade of the chapel.

Soon it would be time to go home but I couldn't be bothered to move. I pulled my tie free and stuffed it into my pocket, rested my head on the wall. When I closed my eyes I became aware of the organ playing inside, the next service beginning. I pictured the minister dabbing at his neck with a handkerchief, reading the same sermon again. He had called my grandmother Elizabeth Agnes, and then just Elizabeth, which wasn't her name, not what my grandfather called her. And later, when the prayers were finished, he had made a long speech about the importance of going to church. Mum and Dad appeared not to be listening, but my sister had tutted beside me, raised her eyebrows when I looked round. She was seven months pregnant and sitting with knees splayed, her hands cupped round her belly. In the aisle at her side I saw my grandfather shake his head as he stared at the coffin. Gran had always worked in her allotment on Sundays, she never had any time for religion. Mum had told that to the minister when he'd called at our house with his hymn book.

My brother came late to the funeral. When I had returned from feeding the pig that morning I heard my mother shouting in the kitchen, Dad's voice trying to calm her. Her eyes were swollen and red, and as I came through the door she swung around sharply, ready to strike me. Her arm fell by her side and my father said quietly, 'Your bathwater's ready, son.' Mum stood by the cooker, glaring at space. When I came down later she was rearranging the living room furniture.

I walked quickly past her and into the kitchen. Dad was making sandwiches. He pulled the slices of bread from their cellophane wrapper and spread them thinly with margarine. Another loaf waited on the table, half a dozen tomatoes beside it. I had brought them home from my grandmother's greenhouse, ripened them on the window sill. As I came to the sink Dad gave me a packet of ham and took a sharp knife from the drawer. 'Don't cut the tomatoes too thick,' he told me. I sat in his chair by the table. Through the open door I could see my mother dusting the sideboard and ornaments, puffing up cushions and setting them nicely. She repositioned the chairs and unwound the flex on the hoover. She had done exactly the same things the previous evening, after the minister had left us.

When the drone of the hoover started again I said to my father, 'So what's up with her?'

Dad wiped his hands on a tea-towel. 'Richard hasn't been home yet,' he said.

He finally appeared halfway through the service. I nudged my sister and whispered, 'Here's Richard now,' and we craned to look over our shoulders. Mum turned with us. He was standing alone in the arch of the doorway, red-faced and unshaven, his thick grey overcoat unbuttoned. An old lady approached him and he bowed his head to look at her hymn sheet. Sunlight streamed through the high windows above them.

The small chapel was crowded and many of the old people were standing. Some of the women carried raincoats, others kept on their headscarves. They might have popped in on their way to the shops, curious to see who had died. A few of them were weeping. I noticed that many of the men wore blazers like Grandad's, the same silver crest on their pockets. It was the club he had gone to with Gran. Outside they shook hands and gathered round his wheelchair, talking in low voices. For a while I stood with them, conscious of my brother behind me, but when I sensed that Richard was going to speak I walked away to the wreaths. I didn't suppose he would follow me.

The names on the cards were mostly familiar, though I couldn't match them to faces. They were old neighbours and workmates, people my grandparents spoke of. I read each message in turn. *Sadly missed* said one, *God bless* another, the same old-fashioned handwriting. Then towards the end of the display I found a bouquet raised up on a bank of white stones. It was addressed to *The best Gran in the world* and signed with my name. The card was edged with pink and blue flowers. Beneath the inscription were three lines of x's. I crouched down and ran my finger over the words. It wasn't my writing, but Mum's, and she hadn't told me she was going to send it.

Richard said, 'She was a good old girl, your gran.'

His shadow lay over the wreaths. Before I looked round I wiped my nose with the back of my hand. There was a graze on the side of my brother's face, dark shadows under his eyes. As I stood up he tugged his shirt collar and loosened his tie. 'Too fucking hot for a funeral anyway,' he said. His shoes were brand new, already scuffed at the toes.

'So take your coat off.'

He shrugged, looked down at the wreaths.

I said, 'She was your gran as well.'

'Yeah.' He rolled a hand over his stubble, made room for an old man to walk past us. Then he said, 'I suppose this lot are coming back to our place.'

'Not all of them.'

'Right.' He nodded. We stood shoulder to shoulder and looked across to the chapel. Light glinted from the windscreens in the car park. I saw my father amongst a group of other men. He was smoking a cigarette. As he flicked some ash to the gravel he rocked back on his heels, mouth open and smiling. Someone was telling a story.

Richard said, 'How are you getting on with the pig anyway?'

I waited. Two elderly ladies were coming towards us, one frail and hunched over, holding the other's arm. 'The pig's okay,' I said.

'You spend enough time out there.'

'Not really.' I went twice a day, after breakfast and in the evening.

'Reckon you'll breed her?' he said. 'Might make a few bob.'

I glanced at his face, tried to read his expression. I couldn't be sure if he was serious. 'I doubt it,' I said finally. By the door of the chapel the minister was talking to Mum. He was holding her hands, his head inclined to one side. I said, 'The pig's ancient.'

'You never know,' said Richard.

'*You* don't,' I said.

My brother grinned, ducked a shoulder towards me. 'I'll tell you what I do know though. I know a guy down the cattle market.' He winked. 'Good price for bacon, Danny.'

I looked in his eyes. 'You're very funny,' I said.

'Yeah.' He pulled open his coat, slipped his hands in his pockets. 'Quality act.'

'Some act,' I said.

Richard ignored me. A large group of people were threading their way past the wreaths, my sister amongst them. She looked very tired, her face almost white above a black smock. Richard waited until she came closer and then called out her name. Several faces looked in our direction. Rachael pursed her lips to prevent herself smiling, shook her head slowly. I said, 'I suppose that's where you were last night, Richard, down the cattle market.' He glanced at me quickly, and I said, 'That's just about your level.'

'No mate, better than that.' He grinned at Rachael, and

as I made to edge past him he held my arm tightly. 'Much better,' he said.

I pulled away, backing over some flowers. 'Bollocks,' I said.

He flashed a smile, turned to reach an arm around Rachael. As I walked away he called cheerfully, 'Catch you later then, Danny.'

His grip still burned on my arm as I stood at the rear of the hall. Inside the chapel the organ was silent. In the distance the workman was preparing to leave, pulling a vest over his head. His white hat sat on the engine of the lawnmower. I dusted my hands on my trousers and pushed myself from the wall. Car doors were slamming at the front of the chapel. Mum's heels clacked over the pavement, stopped where the shadow met sunshine. She said nothing, but waited, her eyes shielded by a pair of dark glasses. I folded my arms over my chest and followed her back to the car, climbed in next to Richard as she went to the front seat. 'That's us both in the shit,' he said, smiling. He hugged his overcoat round his chest.

SIX

WHEN WE first moved to our estate it had been impossible to tell one house from the next. The buildings were laid out in L-shapes and squares and joined together like the parts of a puzzle. Narrow passageways led between them. All the fronts had been whitewashed and the doors painted grey. The roofs were flat. In every square there was a single house of one storey called a bungalow unit where the old people lived, and at the centre of the estate, near the precinct, there were blocks of flats six and seven floors high. In summer the estate became like a playground. We used to race through the alleys and squares as if in a maze, gradually finding our way by the difference in curtains and ornaments. At that time I was in primary school, my sister about to leave secondary. Now most of the houses closest to ours had been bought from the Council and their exteriors repainted or cladded, narrow extensions built onto front doors. The newspaper said the prices were cheap, but despite Rachael's advice my parents were not interested in buying; they said it was safer to rent, the leaking roof was due for repair. Next door the bungalow unit was empty and boarded.

Before we left for the funeral Mum drew the blinds at the front and back of the living room. She didn't want the neighbours looking in. She had washed the blinds the previous week and the smell of disinfectant had lingered for days. Now the room smelled of old ladies' perfume, drinks and tobacco. There were more people than we expected. They were drinking sherry and whisky, eating Dad's sandwiches. Mum eased between them with a plate in each hand, smiling for everyone. Dad offered refills. For a while I sat close to my grandfather and shook hands with his friends. They made jokes about getting lost in the estate, said the house was roomier inside than they expected. But they avoided talking about my grandmother. Some of the women bent down to kiss Grandad, and one lady also tried to kiss me, but I flinched away from her. She gave a laugh. 'He must be saving himself, Joe!'

'Oh, he's innocent yet,' Grandad said. He touched my knee and I rose to let the woman sit down. She rubbed my cheek. Her fingers were dry.

'You are kind,' she said. Then louder to Grandad. 'He takes after his grandfather, Joe, a proper young gentleman.'

'Better looking, Sadie,' he replied, but his smile faded quickly. The old woman smoothed the side of her skirt and made herself comfortable. Her eyes were bright; she wore a ring on each of her fingers. I looked to the other side of the room and found myself staring at Rachael.

Although we had entered the chapel together, and sat side by side, we had not spoken more than a few words. I had questions I wanted to ask her, but when we'd returned from the service she had seemed more interested in Richard. They had disappeared for several minutes to the garden, came indoors when my mother sent Dad outside to fetch them. Now Richard was in the kitchen and my sister was listening to an old man in a blazer, bending slightly fowards to hear him. Behind them the sun glowed dully through the blinds, glinted along the top slats. Their faces appeared very red. When the man started to laugh Rachael smiled thinly and took a sip from her glass. Then she glanced in my direction and raised her eyebrows. I decided to cross the room, turned round to tell Grandad. Sadie was holding his hand. She rubbed it softly between hers. 'You'll be glad of your family anyway,' she said. 'They'll be taking good care of you.'

He frowned. 'But I've digs with the Council, Sadie,' he said. 'I'm staying in the Home up on Beatrice Road. Did ye not know?'

'I didn't know, no,' she said carefully. There was a pause and she added. 'No, I didn't know that, but they do say the Beatrice is a lovely place, Joe, a real three-star affair.'

Grandad nodded but didn't reply, and I said, 'It's just an emergency stay.'

An ambulance had fetched him the day after Gran died. It said *Social Services* on the side doors. There was a lift at the back for his wheelchair, several other old people inside. A young woman had draped Grandad's knees beneath a white blanket and had spoken as if he was deaf, as if to a child. He hadn't complained; he hadn't said anything. Mum had followed from the cottage with a few of his things wrapped inside a dressing gown.

I said to Sadie, 'We're going to see if he can move in next door.' I gestured in Rachael's direction. 'My sister's husband works for the Council. He's going to arrange it.'

Sadie leaned closer to Grandad and squeezed his arm. 'That'll be convenient for you, Joe, next door.'

'Aye.' He nodded, felt in his lap for his cigarettes. 'But they've been awfy kind to me in the Home, Sadie. Good grub, clean sheets. Ye couldnae ask for cleaner accommodation.' His hands were unsteady and he fumbled as he opened the pack. One cigarette fell to the floor, he placed another between his lips. I took the matches from him and struck a light as he leaned forwards. He said, 'Because I'm an old man now, d'ye see? I cannae be doing with all that.'

'You don't want the trouble, no,' said Sadie.

I crouched down and lifted the cigarette from the carpet. I said, 'We're going to have the bungalow converted. It's a bit of a dump.' But Sadie was looking at Grandad. 'The one next door,' I added. His eyes were moist, gazing into the room. Sadie reached again for his hand. Blue smoke wound from his nose.

As I picked a way through the crowd to my sister I transferred the cigarette from my hand to my shirt pocket, twisting away from where my mother was standing. The voices around me were cheerful and a group of people near Rachael were laughing. The old man in the blazer touched her arm, talking eagerly, almost shouting. I stood quietly beside them. The man was describing his family. He was smaller than both of us. 'I had fourteen brothers and sisters,' he said. 'Fourteen I knew, and one sister I never did see. She emigrated to Canada in 1902, and that's where she died. Because there was a baby born nearly every year, you see, and that's how it went on, they had one a year and didn't know the difference. I was the youngest,' he said, 'and I'm seventy-eight next birthday.'

Rachael said, 'Your poor mother.' She caught my eye and I smiled.

'Yes and no,' the man said. He jigged his hand from side

to side, glancing at both of us. 'It was hard of course – they were ignorant times and there was a lot more children that didn't make it. I had a twin brother who died. He was three months and they tell me he was buried in a grocery crate.'

The man smiled, and Rachael said, 'How awful.'

'It was,' he agreed. 'But then in later years, you see, she always had her family around her. So she never went short, not in that respect. She was never lacking for company.'

'No,' Rachael said.

'You ask old Joe,' the man said to me. 'He'll remember.' I nodded; the man looked at Rachael's belly. 'But that's all in the past,' he said then, 'and good riddance too.'

My sister sipped at her drink. 'It's interesting,' she said.

'They were interesting times,' he replied. 'But what about you, dear? This won't be your first, I know.'

'Third,' said Rachael. 'Third and last.'

'Girl or boy?' the man demanded. He leaned forwards, his mouth slightly open.

'Boy this time, we hope.'

'Yes,' he said, sinking back. 'A boy to finish off, and that'll do nicely.' He lowered his voice slightly, edged closer. 'Because the big families are long gone,' he told us. 'At least among our kind. Now my mother was Irish, so that explains the carry on here, but it's the Pakistanis you want to watch out for these days. They're the ones.' He nodded. 'That's right, isn't it, son – watch out for the pakis?'

'No,' I said, and felt myself flushing. I turned towards Rachael. There was a smile in her eyes. I said casually, 'Has Tom seen about the bungalow yet, Rachael?'

She wrinkled her brow, gave a small shake of her head. After a moment she said, 'Which bungalow, Danny?'

'Next door to here.'

Rachael smiled an apology to the old man, and he said,

'That's all right, dear, you carry on.' He was trying to be helpful. He pulled open his blazer and slipped his hands in his trouser pockets, parted his feet a few inches. He jangled his keys. My cheeks were burning. I said, 'Tom was going to see about getting the bungalow for Grandad. He said he'd let me know this weekend.' She looked at me blankly. 'I was wondering if you knew anything.'

'Nothing at all,' she said. She drank from her glass, briefly widened her mouth to a smile. 'Sorry.'

I said, 'Forget it,' and looked over my shoulder. I sensed the old man was thinking of something to say, that Rachael was annoyed, though I couldn't think why. Like my mother, she took offence easily, without reason, and her disagreements with Tom were always mysterious, private between them. I sighed heavily and ducked past the old man, pushed through to the kitchen.

Richard straightened from the fridge as I came through the door. He was holding a beer can. As he pulled back the ring-pull his beer frothed over the rim and spattered the floor. He held the can away from his body and shook his free hand. The back door was open. A couple of flies turned in the sunshine. I pulled out a chair and kicked off my shoes. 'So where were you?' I said.

'Come again?'

'Where were you last night?'

He sucked the beer from his fingers. 'My business,' he said.

I looked under the table for my trainers. 'Mum went crazy,' I said.

'Mum always does.' He stepped to the door and tossed the ring-pull into the grass. He patted his pockets and took out his cigarettes, 'Want one?' he said.

I looked up, tugging a trainer over my heel. 'Three,' I told him.

Richard tossed a single cigarette to the table and bent to light his own from the cooker. He leant against the worktop, blew a column of smoke at the ceiling. It was not unusual for him to stay out overnight, but usually he came home during breakfast, sometimes as Mum was leaving for work. He rarely said where he had been. He did not like to be questioned. What I knew about him I had learned from listening to his conversations on the telephone or the doorstep, the few things Rachael told me, clues that I found in his bedroom. Sometimes his absences from home were longer, and then he would say he had been looking for work. Once he had disappeared to London for six months, found a job in a hotel kitchen. Mum thought he had rejoined the army.

I said, 'Meet anyone interesting?'

Richard smiled to himself, glanced at me sideways. I dropped the cigarette in my shirt pocket, began tying my laces. He said, 'I did as a matter of fact. I bumped into Tom outside the chinky.' A sparrow hopped across Dad's patio. I stamped my foot and it startled, flew over the fence. 'You know you don't stand a chance with that bungalow, Danny?' he said.

I looked round sharply. 'Did Tom say that?'

'Tom doesn't need to. The place is a pigsty, Danny, let's face it. It's not fit for anything.' I shrugged, pressed my lips firmly together. He said, 'Besides which, Tom's a nobody. He doesn't have the authority anyway.'

'Listen to you,' I said. I crossed to the sink and bent to drink from the tap. Richard waited. As I wiped my mouth he said, 'How's that, Danny?'

'If Tom's a nobody, what does that make you?' I moved to the doorway, felt the sun on my neck, the back of my head.

Richard drank slowly from his can. He smiled. 'Not a

pen-pusher anyway,' he said. He used the can to tap himself on the chest. 'Queen and country, mate. One of the few.'

I said, 'You were a chef. Big deal.'

'Fucking good one, mind you.' He was joking. I glanced at the clock and stepped backwards onto the patio, pulled the door shut between us. Richard shook his head through the window, still smiling, and when I glanced back from the gate he raised his can, took a long drag on his cigarette.

SEVEN

OUTSIDE THE heat was stifling. I loosened my shirt and turned from our gate, hurrying between high fences. Sunlight filtered through the slats and the wood gave off a smell of warm creosote. From the windows of the houses beyond came the sound of music and sports programmes, a low murmur of voices. I heard a woman suddenly shouting, a pot slammed hard on a cooker. Then a baby began to wail. At the end of the row I entered a passageway and emerged to a square of houses almost identical to ours. There were burglar alarms beneath the upstairs windows, bright red and yellow boxes. We also had one, brought home from Dad's work and never connected. A small group of children lay face down on the concrete, drawing pictures of spacemen with blue and green crayons. I stepped around them and crossed to the next passageway, out through a complex of garages and into an older estate.

Here the houses had chimneys, red-tiled roofs and bay windows. I found a low wall and sat down, tugged my shirt free of my belt. I rolled up my sleeves. Towards the end of the street a woman in wellingtons was washing her car. A stream of white soapy water ran by the side of the kerb and into a drain. For a while I watched her, the curve of her breasts in her T-shirt. Then she picked up her bucket and walked to the far side of the car. Standing on tip-toe she emptied the water over the roof and something in the tightness of her face told me she knew I was looking. Before she glanced up I leant my arms on my knees and pretended to be absorbed in the pavement.

A swarm of tiny red insects crawled round my feet. I drew back my heels and left two pink streaks in the concrete. One summer, a long time before, Richard had shown me how to make a flame-thrower from an aerosol can. With another boy I had spent an afternoon at this spot, scorching insects, until an old lady had come from the house opposite to chase us away. She kept our matches. Her name was Janet and she wore her hair in a tall silver bun. When she died my grandparents went to her funeral, and the house had stood empty for months. Now an Indian family lived there.

As I watched I saw Surinder briefly appear at an upstairs window, half-hidden by lace curtains. I counted to sixty and the front door opened. She wore jeans and shiny gold sandals, her anorak unzipped over a T-shirt. As she crossed the street she glanced over towards me, almost smiling, and I turned to see her disappear into the estate where I lived. She was carrying a plastic shopping bag and her hair was loose, over her shoulders. I yawned and stretched out my arms, stood slowly, and followed her.

Deeper into the estate the buildings became taller, surrounded by scaffolding. Wooden boards blanked out the windows and most of the walls had been sprayed with graffiti. Men in blue overalls worked on the skyline. They arrived in vans from the south every day except Sunday and they spoke with loud London accents. Huge metal skips sat in each of the squares and the air seemed filled with pale yellow dust. I hurried through passageways littered with rubble until I arrived at a wide open concourse, the shopping precinct. Here too the windows were boarded, and the boards protected by grilles. From the open door of a pub came the smell of beer and cigarette smoke, the clatter of a fruit machine. When the steelworks had closed a lot of the shops had gone out of business and now there was only the supermarket. It belonged to Surinder's father. On the pavement outside a bin lay upended, spilling a trail of bottles and cans. A small dog rooted around in the rubbish, its tail wagging stiffly. I felt in my pocket for change and entered the shop.

As I glanced upwards I saw myself framed on a television screen, passing the vegetables. The black-and-white monitor was attached to the ceiling, and beneath it sat a woman called Marjory. She was reading the wrapper of a chocolate bar. She placed it next to the till and took a breath and waited to serve me. Mr Sidhu sat at the far end of the aisles, behind the meat counter, his hands on his knees. I laid a bag of crisps before Marjory and asked for some matches. She reached lazily to the rack at her side and opened her palm for my money. As she returned my change she said, 'Thanking you,' and looked away to the door. Mr Sidhu nodded minutely from his chair.

Outside I sat down on the edge of a tree-pot, a large concrete tub decorated with graffiti. There were half a dozen or so. The trees were dead, thin silhouettes, and their bark was stripped bare. I called to the dog and emptied the crisps at my feet. Close by a small boy was drawing patterns on his plimsolls with a biro. Behind him on the wall there was a triangular plaque, an architectural award. Once our estate had been famous. I said, 'Is this your dog then?' The boy came and stood closer. He shook his head. I tickled behind the dog's ear.

'We had a cat once,' he said.

'Yeah?'

'It got put to sleep.'

'How come?'

The boy grinned. 'My dad killed it.' He shifted his weight from one foot to the other and scratched at his belly. 'Can I get some crisps?'

I let the empty packet fall from my hand. 'All gone,' I said.

He paused for a moment, looked over his shoulder. He seemed anxious, uncertain. 'I'm going now,' he said.

'Okay.'

He left hesitantly, then charged at a sprint through a passageway. His footsteps continued to echo long after he'd gone. I went in the other direction, around the side of the supermarket.

Although our estate was on the edge of the town it had no exit to the countryside. The road which brought the lorries and vans to the rear of the shops looped around in a horseshoe from an older estate. Narrow side roads led off to car parks and garages. Three times every hour a small bus arrived from the town centre and waited at the back of the precinct. It always travelled in a clockwise direction. As I crossed to the next block of housing I glanced at the stop and recognized a girl from my school. I waved but she didn't respond.

The houses on the other side of the road were coloured

grey and blue, and had different shaped porches, but the pattern of squares and alleys was identical to ours. I walked quickly. Where the buildings ended there was a tall grassy bank topped by a row of spindly trees. Rubbish had gathered in a ditch at the foot of the slope; a shopping trolley lay on its side. I clambered to the top, clutching at grass, and ducked through the trees. A wide shimmering road stood before me, the dual carriageway which led to the steelworks and my grandparents' cottage. A water tower stood on the horizon to my right, bright against the blue sky. Few heavy lorries passed this way now and the road was often empty in both directions. When the cars came they sped past in threes and fours, growling into the distance. In the silence they left you could hear the gulls over the fields, tractors and insects. A metal barrier ran the line of the kerb. In its shadow I saw the flattened carcass of a rabbit. There was a hub-cap further along. I stepped onto the tarmac and crossed slowly. The slope on the far side was gentler and longer, falling to a brook, trees and farmlands beyond. Half way down Surinder was waiting. I called her name and waded through the long grass to meet her.

EIGHT

SURINDER CHEWED on the end of a grass stalk and stared out to the fields. Cows dotted a meadow; there was a solitary house in the distance, a few scattered outbuildings. An aeroplane left a white trail in the sky. When she took the stalk from her mouth she used it to point with, and said, 'Maybe that's where he lives, Danny.'

I lay back in the grass, pillowing my head in my arms. 'Where who lives?' I asked her.

'The farmer.' She brought her face closer. Her eyes were large, heavy-lidded. The outward curve of her nose touched mine.

'Bound to,' I said. 'It's a farm.'

'The one your Gran went to.' As I closed my eyes I felt her shadow moving across me. She sat on my thighs, made herself comfortable. She tickled my chin with the stalk. 'What do you think?'

I said, 'Maybe. I don't know.' I flicked at the stalk but kept my eyes closed. Surinder became silent, and I said, 'Maybe we should go and see.' I squinted at her silhouette.

She trailed the stalk round my face, tossed it away to one side. 'If you like,' she said.

Sometimes the farmer had visited my grandparents' cottage with parcels of meat, but he didn't come into the house. Whilst Gran went to search for her purse he had waited on the back doorstep and bellowed his news to Grandad inside. He called them Mr and Mrs Erskine and referred to himself by his first name. 'Take it from Ted, Mr Erskine,' he shouted. 'You take it from Ted.' One winter Gran had persuaded him indoors for a whisky. I was six years old and soon it would be Christmas. Outside it was snowing. On a sheet of newspaper by the fireplace I was arranging a collection of coal lumps in order of size and my hands and face were smeared with coal dust. Before I could escape Ted had stooped to lift me high in the air. And behind him, a long way below, I could see my grandmother smiling, holding a parcel, the paper stained pink. Ted called me his piccaninny and he shook me as my father would do. But he wasn't angry. A bush of hairs grew wildly from each nostril, trembling as he laughed. Snow lay on his shoulders and cap, his hands felt cold and damp through my pyjamas. When I began to cry he lowered me gently and rubbed at my shoulder. Then he laughed again and sat down. I climbed onto my grandfather's knee and stayed there until Ted went from the house. In later years he appeared less often, though Gran continued to walk to his farm when she had to. A younger man came to deliver the meat. He brought pig-feed and bales of hay, took the pigs away when it was time to collect them. I had no idea where they were taken.

Surinder tugged lightly on my shirt pocket. 'Did you get any fags?' she asked me.

'Two,' I said. 'And I got some matches from Marjory.' I watched as she fished in my pocket. She lit both the cigarettes and placed one in my mouth, flicked the match to the grass. I propped myself on my elbow. 'Do you want to see the pig then?'

Surinder lifted her face and blew a long cloud of smoke at the sky. Her mouth was small, the top lip upturned, a faint shadow above it. I wanted to kiss her. She said, 'I suppose so. I don't know.'

'They've got bellies like ours you know. The digestive system is exactly the same, their guts and stuff.'

'Yours maybe,' she said, and shifted her weight.

I puffed on my cigarette. The smoke tasted sour and made my head spin. I lay flat in the grass, felt the ground tilting gently beneath me. When I closed my eyes it went faster. I said quietly, 'She's not dirty you know. She's sweet. You'll like her.'

Surinder's voice said, 'Does she have a name yet?'

'Doesn't need one,' I murmured.

'What if she was a dog? Or a goldfish?'

I listened to the sound of my breathing. 'You don't eat dogs,' I said.

'But you're not going to eat the pig either.'

I didn't answer, kept my eyes closed; and Surinder pinched me. 'Are you?' she insisted.

'No,' I said. I was smiling.

'So give it a name.'

'Like what?'

'Like something beginning with A, for instance.'

'Anna Banana,' I said.

'Okay.'

'You're joking.' I looked up through narrowed eyes. The sun shimmered in the outline of her hair; her face against the bright sky was featureless. 'You've got split ends,' I told her.

Surinder blew a column of smoke in my face and poked at my stomach. I let my cigarette fall to the grass, waited until she looked away. Then I grabbed for her sides, the soft flesh of her waist. She gave out a scream and twisted away from me, digging her nails in my arm. As she fell fowards her hair covered my face, smelling of coconut. She was screaming and giggling. I tried to clutch harder, but the effort was too much, I was too hot. When I let go she sagged forwards and lay on top of me, breathing in gasps, still giggling. My cheek and ears were burning and I had an erection.

For a long time we lay motionless. I could feel my pulse racing, Surinder's heart pounding against me. Tentatively I slipped my hands beneath her waistband, tucked them inside her knickers. 'When do you have to get back?' I whispered.

'I'm at the library,' she said.

Her plastic bag lay beside us, a bright picture of vegetables and fruit in the grass. The hard shape of the books inside reminded me of school, empty classrooms and corridors, the last day of term. On our final afternoon the headmaster had called our group to his office. He gave us each a green badge. We were special, he told us, the doctors and teachers and engineers of the future. He sat down on the edge of his desk, arms folded and smiling. He waited as his secretary pushed through a trolley of biscuits and coffee. She smiled at Surinder, left quietly, and when she had gone the headmaster leaned suddenly forwards, clasping his hands. A levels were the sensible course, he said, university was not beyond us. We fingered our badges as he described his own career, how he came to be a head teacher. He began as a prefect, he told us, it was a long time ago. I dropped my badge in my pocket, watched through the window as the classrooms emptied onto the playground. When finally the headmaster rose to open his door there was no one in sight; the only sound came from the cleaners upstairs. He shook us each by the hand as we filed past him. 'Use the holidays wisely,' he said. 'Fresh air and study.' At home I kicked my books under the bed and switched on the radio. Two days later Gran died.

Surinder lifted her head from my shoulder and I saw she was smirking.

'What is it?'

She pressed her forehead against mine. 'You've got a hard-on.'

Her lips were warm and moist and I kept my eyes open. Her eyelashes flickered, a tiny speck of black powder trembled on one eyelid. I pushed my hands deeper into her jeans, until I was stretching, and Surinder pressed herself more firmly against me. Then suddenly her mouth left me. She gripped my wrists in her hands. 'Race you down the hill!' she said.

'Surinder!'

I descended slowly. At the foot of the slope she pulled off her sandals and hitched up her jeans. The brook was perfectly still. A faint stagnant smell rose to meet us and insects hung over the surface, darting abruptly. As Surinder stepped into the water an oily film parted in loops round her ankles, glistening like tinfoil. I stood on the bank and watched her, keeping my hands in my pockets. I could still feel the impression of her body against mine.

Surinder shivered and crossed her arms over her chest, one hand on each shoulder. She bent forwards. 'It's freezing!' she cried.

'It stinks,' I said.

As she waded away I followed some yards behind, dragging my feet through the grass. Brief swirling eddies chased the back of her legs, brought clouds of sediment to the surface. She found a stick on the bank and drew it through the water. Then she glanced at me, and said, 'I don't mind you know.'

I looked at her. She stood still. 'About what?'

'Your hands, that sort of thing.' She pursed her lips. The tip of the stick broke the surface of the water, three rings spreading outwards. 'What we said yesterday.'

'What did we say yesterday?' My heart was beating very fast. I wanted to sit down, or carry on walking, talk about something different. She looked at me sharply and I glanced away, fixed my gaze on the water upstream. I saw a dragonfly, midges, a sudden plop in the centre of the brook. Surinder turned and clambered up the opposite bank. With her face obscured by her hair she sat down in the grass, tucked her legs underneath her. Suddenly she hurled her stick at the water.

'You know what we said!' She pulled up a dandelion and began to tear it to pieces.

I sat down, and waited a long time, my chin on one knee. Then I said, 'We could go to Grandad's house.'

Surinder twisted the stem of the dandelion round her finger. She didn't reply.

'If you want to,' I said.

There was a pause, and she said quietly, without looking up, 'You know I do. I said so yesterday.'

I fought an impulse to smile. 'You said maybe,' I told her.

Her voice was quieter still, spoken to the dandelion. 'Not maybe. What I said wasn't maybe.'

'What was it then?'

'Stop teasing, Danny.' She threw the curled stem to the brook. It floated on the surface, slowly unwinding. We watched it.

'I'd better go then,' I said. Surinder nodded, looked down. 'Will I see you tomorrow? Here?'

She tossed back her hair, stretched her legs in the grass. Dirt had gathered between her toes. She flexed them, and said, 'Maybe,' not grinning.

I hesitated, pushed my hands in my pockets. I turned to go and then stopped. 'We'll call the pig Agnes,' I said.

'Agnes!'

I nodded, smiling, and began to climb up the slope. 'My gran's name,' I shouted. 'Agnes.'

NINE

GRANDAD SAID, 'Will ye take a drop of whisky, son? Before ye go?'

I said I would, although he knew I didn't much like it. There was a bottle on his bedside cabinet, two small glasses beside it. I passed them across. Through the open window behind me I could hear the women shouting in the kitchens below, a row of ovens clanking shut, someone laughing. Grandad's alarm clock read a quarter to twelve, almost his dinner time. He handed me a glass and lit another cigarette. His hands were shaking and he squinted before drinking.

'Aye, son,' he said then, 'that was one of your gran's sayings about the pigs – *what they cannae turn tae meat they turn tae shite!*' He raised his eyebrows and chuckled. The bed creaked beneath him. I sipped at my drink. In the week since my grandmother died he had described many times how he found her that morning, but he rarely mentioned her name without weeping. On the bedspread beside him lay a wrinkled grey handkerchief. He bunched it in his fist and dabbed at his eyes, then said, 'But that's the only thing for it, Danny. Spread a wee bit on the garden tae keep the veg happy, and dump the rest in the cutting.' He mimed the action. 'Nae other bugger will want it.'

'No,' I agreed. The whisky burned in my throat, settled warm on my stomach. I rolled the glass in my palms and said, 'Seems a shame to waste it though.'

'Right enough, son,' he said. 'But we had a use for it at one time, ye know.' He gestured with his cigarette at the window. 'All the neighbours there, they used tae come along with their table scraps, when we kept the two pigs. And sometimes we kept more than that – I mind there were four pigs the year Richard was born, and we never spent two bob tae feed them. We did a swap, d'ye see? The neighbours chipped in with their scraps and they got a pile of shite in return! Manure for the gardens. Because most folk kept a wee patch at that time. It wasnae just your gran had the green fingers, Danny.' He leaned forwards and touched my knee with his glass. 'Then at Christmas we gave them each a wee joint for the pot. Aye. Because they were good people in them days, helped one another.'

He drank and for several minutes he was silent. I gazed over my shoulder. His window gave a view of the courtyard at the rear of the Home, and beyond that a graveyard. In the shade of the bins immediately below there were two empty deckchairs, a dog fast asleep. On the long hill of the cemetery I could see a man in his shirtsleeves, polishing a gravestone. His jacket and cap were draped from the arm of a stone crucifix.

I said, 'How come you kept the four pigs that time, Grandad?'

He shook his head vaguely and frowned. 'I cannae mind now, son. It was your gran used to decide these things, no me. She went across tae Ted's at the back of every New Year – used tae walk it, every year without fail. And then he drove her back in his lorry, his old jalopy, with the pigs up there in the back. I mind she used tae sit beside him in the cabin, feart for her life. Because it was a hand-knitted old thing, so it was. Wonder tae me it wasnae horse drawn.' He looked for my smile, and went on, 'Then when it came to the slaughter Ted fetched them back again. Same routine if your gran decided to breed them, Ted drove the wagon across with the boar in the back. But why she kept the four that year, I cannae tell ye, son.'

He sucked on his cigarette, stubbed it weakly in the ashtray. A trolley rattled along the corridor outside, cups chinking, and a little while after there was a knock at the door. A girl's face appeared, red from the sun, and I looked at the floor. 'Dinner now, Joe,' she said.

She left the door ajar, and Grandad said, 'Did I ever tell ye about the wee sheeny two doors along from us, son?'

'No,' I said, though I knew the story well. He was a singer.

'Jewish,' said Grandad. 'He came from the Ukraine originally, a DP ye know. Came over here at the end of the war with his missus, and she was a helluva nice wee soul. Used tae come chat with Agnes when I was away, sit blethering for hours in the kitchen there. 'Good day, Mr Erskine,' she used tae say. 'Good day, Mr Erskine.' Never Joe. Agnes was Agnes, but in all the years I knew her she never once cried me Joe. And the wee fella and her, every Sunday night they had their chums over, and Christ, singers! Like nightingales. I tell ye, we sat there one night – it was summer, this time of year, grand weather – and we were listening to the radio, the wireless – nae television in them days. And I says to your gran, 'Here Agnes, turn that bugger off a minute.' So we opened the front door and we sat in the dark for nigh on three hours, just soaking it up. Because it was beautiful, so it was. Couldnae understand a word of it, mind, but the voices – jeez, it was the best turn ye ever heard in your life!' Grandad placed his free hand on his hip and puffed out his chest. 'He was only a wee fella mind, but strong! He had a chest on him like a wash tub and he used tae lift the steel tubes like they was firewood. Strong as a crane and a voice like an angel. But,' he took a last drink from his glass, 'he was no much of a gardener. He was out there every night after his shift, singing away to the cabbages, but they never did grow for him. He used tae send a lot of his stuff along to your gran. Sent it over with his missus, for the pigs. We gave him all the pigshite he wanted, but he wouldnae take any meat off us. Against the religion, d'ye see? Pork. Well, "Suits me," I used to say. "That'll do me." Oh, I liked my grub. Still do!'

He patted his belly, made a sign for me to bring over his wheelchair. With trembling arms he heaved his body into the seat and loosened the brakes. I gave him his cigarettes and matches.

'So how are they taking care of ye downstairs, Danny?'

I gripped the handles of his chair and pushed him to the door. 'Okay,' I said. Each day when I came I took a plastic tub to the kitchens. The cook had been a friend of my gran's; she filled the tub with leftover food, teased me in front of the other women.

'And I'll be seeing ye tomorrow then, son?'

'Same time,' I said. 'I'll bring some fruit up, Mum's getting some.'

'Nae apples, mind.' He pushed out his false teeth on his tongue and winked at me. When I started to laugh he pressed some notes into my hand.

I wheeled him along a dimly lit corridor and into the dining area. A place had been set at one of the tables where three old ladies were already eating. When the first saw him she put down her fork and spooned some potatoes onto his plate. Another poured out his tea. Despite the food there was a smell of disinfectant and urine, as there was everywhere in the building. The old people ate in near silence and when Grandad spoke a few words several of them looked up expectantly.

I left him to eat and walked through the television lounge for the exit. Away from his room I became conscious of the wide open spaces around me and I lengthened my stride. From the doorway of another dining area an old man raised his hand, as he had done the previous day. His white hair was tangled and his eyes were glazed over. Gravy dribbled from one side of his mouth. I called out a greeting and turned onto the stairs, jumping four at a time, rattling the bannister. The matron looked out from her office and smiled. A man was making a delivery of beer. I edged past him and hurried around the side of the building to the kitchens. There was ten pounds in my pocket.

TEN

O N THE Sunday after the funeral I had waited on the grass bank for almost an hour, watching the clouds drifting over, listening for movement. Cows grazed in the distance, a few cars passed on the road, but Surinder didn't appear. When it began to turn cold I got up and walked home. I took a route around the backs of the houses in the hope that I would see her. A few children ran past me, wearing suits and party frocks. An old man in slippers whistled to his dog from a corner. But I saw no one else. In my bedroom I lay down on the quilt with a schoolbook and turned the pages at random, unable to concentrate. I smoked both our cigarettes and imagined she was stretched out beside me. She smiled as I told her about my parents, my brother, the plans I had for the cottage. But when I tried to picture what we did next she was no longer there, I couldn't remember the shape of her face, or how she felt when I touched her. I draped myself in the quilt and kicked off my shoes, thinking of the woman washing her car, the curve of her breasts in her T-shirt.

In the evening, when I returned from feeding the pig, I found that my bed had been made and the windows left open. The room still smelled of cigarettes. I took a book from under my bed and tried to fan the stale air from my room, but it was pointless, already too late. When I went downstairs to the kitchen my mother looked at me coolly, and asked if I would like one of her cigarettes, offering her packet. She slapped me hard on the face before I could answer. My two stubs sat on the table behind her. Without waiting to hear what she would say I turned and left by the back door, slamming it after me.

The clouds had darkened and a drizzle was falling. I pulled up my collar and walked in the direction of Surinder's. I passed her house slowly and when I was sure that no one was watching I paused and came back, sat down on the wall opposite hers. With my shoulders hunched I stared up at her curtains, willing her to come to the window, determined I wouldn't go home. But when finally she appeared it was from the entrance to the estate. She was coming home with her father. He wore a turban and sandals, his shirt sleeves rolled to the elbows. As they stepped from the kerb he called, 'Terrible weather!' and pointed to the sky, shaking his head. Surinder grimaced and looked down, went into the house ahead of him.

I guessed she had been working in the shop and in the days that followed I avoided having to go there. I didn't know what I would say if she served me, and I was afraid she might be annoyed. Perhaps she had decided against meeting me, perhaps her father suspected. But now I found myself heading in their direction, and walking quickly, not knowing what I would do when I got there. I tried to think of a way to persuade her outside. I could ask her to sell me a biro, then leave and write her a note. Later I could return as if I had forgotten something, bread or cheese, a pint of milk. I could pass the note across when I paid. Then I realized I was carrying no money. As I approached the first square of scaffolding my pace slowed and I stepped beneath the shade of some boards. I sat down on a pile of cement sacks and turned out my pockets. A dead match fell to the ground. A few minutes later I saw her.

She was wearing a grey nylon coat and her hair was pulled back in a pleat. When she recognized me she grinned and made a small curtsy, lifting the hem of the coat. I stepped into the sunlight, shielding my eyes. 'Fat Marjory's sick,' she told me.

We stood slightly apart from each other. In the open space of the square I felt ill at ease and conspicuous. I glanced up at the workmen. 'Till when?' I said.

She shrugged. 'No idea, couple more days maybe.'

'You were supposed to meet me last Sunday.'

'I know.' She slipped her hands in her pockets. 'But Dad said I had to help out in the shop. He thinks I've got nothing better to do. All these trips to the library.'

I poked with my shoe at the pavement. 'You still want to then?'

'Of course! I want to see this pig you're so in love with.'

I said, 'I was down there this morning you know, doing some work in the garden, and guess what? I found a rats' nest.' Surinder's eyes flickered away from me. I said, 'It was in the old compost heap, I was just forking it over and I heard this squeaking noise. It was a nest of babies, all curled up in a circle, little pink things, you could see the veins and everything. They had their eyes closed.' She frowned, glanced past my shoulder. 'So then I went off to find the mother. I looked everywhere, all around the houses and that, in the pigsty, and the greenhouse – they probably came from the tip. What do you think? Should I go back and kill them, the babies?'

But Surinder wasn't listening. I followed her gaze and recognized the two boys called Spider and Stan. They were watching from the shade of a passageway, their shirts tied round their waists. Spider held a bottle of cider. I heard a faint snickering and one of them belched. In a low voice Surinder said, 'They keep coming in the shop but they never buy anything. They just look at you and walk out again.' She bit her lip. 'It gives me the creeps.'

I heard footsteps and motioned towards her. 'We'd better go,' I said. But the boys were already coming towards us. Stan twitched his nose and made a sniffing noise. He placed a hand on my shoulder and smiled at me, twisting to inspect the heel of his boot. 'Funny smell round here,' he said. 'Like dogshit or something.' I bore his weight without moving, arms folded, but flinched as he released me. He raised an eyebrow and grinned. 'Ain't me anyway,' he said.

'What about her?' Spider cradled the bottle. A line of black hair snaked down to his waistband.

'Who?'

'That paki.'

As Stan bent towards her, Surinder moved her weight to one leg and took a long breath, watching him steadily. His face was screwed in disgust and when he pulled away he spat hard at the pavement. 'Jesus wept, man!' he spluttered. 'Pongs like fuck.'

'Like dogshit,' said Spider. He let out a short laugh before drinking, passed the cider to Stan as he began to sway backwards. Surinder tugged at my sleeve.

'Let's go, Danny,' she said, but Spider took hold of my wrist.

'Hold on, mate.' A fringe of dark hair reached down to his eyes and he had to tilt his chin forwards to see me. His eyes were straining to focus. 'I know you,' he said. For the first time I realized he was smaller than me, and the realization made me feel foolish. I cleared my throat but said nothing. The previous summer he had dragged me to the ground as I was crossing the school playground. He had held me by the shoulders as Stan kicked me hard in the stomach and back. Before strolling away they scattered my books over a fence. I hadn't provoked them, and the following day we passed in a corridor as though nothing had happened. Now Spider said, 'You're an arsehole,' but still didn't seem able to place me. Behind him Surinder was waiting, ready to run. At the top of the scaffolding a workman stretched his arms wide, then turned and walked out of sight.

'Would you let us go please,' I said.

Spider shook his head slowly. He hooked a finger into the neck of my shirt, flicked his thumb against the top button. 'Funny guy,' he murmured. 'Fucking comedian.' His breath was sour with cigarettes and drink. I tried to pull myself from his grip and heard my shirt tear. The button came free. For a moment we paused, Spider seeming bewildered, and then Surinder took my hand in hers and dragged me away from him.

We hurried under the scaffolding and into a derelict bungalow, out through the back door to the garden. There was a wheelbarrow in our path. It was spattered with plaster. As Surinder skipped to one side I tried to hurdle the handles, almost fell as I landed. Although the gate was still upright the garden fence had been flattened and the planks were strewn across the children's play area beyond. We ran through a concrete tunnel smelling of urine, ducked beneath a wooden climbing frame, a row of tyres hanging from ropes. Behind us I could hear the boys laughing, but realized they were not following. One of them made a noise like a dog barking. As we passed between two windowless buildings Surinder slowed her pace to match mine and we turned left and right through the squares that surrounded the shopping precinct, finally came to a halt at the bus stop behind the supermarket. I smiled. Surinder was panting. 'So, shall I kill them or what?' I said.

'Them two!'

'The rats.'

She leant over with her hand on her knees until she had caught her breath. 'I ought to stop smoking your cigarettes,' she said. Then straightening she looked along the road in both directions. 'Suppose so,' she said. 'It's up to you.'

The rear of her father's shop had no windows, and the solitary door had no handle or keyhole. It was metal, painted red. Beneath the layer of red I could see the names of Spider and Stan. I nodded at the door. 'Did they upset you?' I asked.

Surinder shrugged. 'They're low-life. Scum.' She stood down from the kerb and stepped backwards into the road. 'Don't worry about it.'

'You should be careful.'

Her eyes met mine and looked away again. 'Here's a bus coming,' she said. Then, 'When shall we go to your cottage?'

'Whenever you like.' I tried to stand aside as she jumped to the kerb. We almost collided. I held her arms briefly, let go as the bus doors flipped open.

'Day after tomorrow,' she said.

'Okay.' I nodded and tried not to grin. Very quickly she kissed me. 'Where are you going?' I said.

Surinder boarded the bus and sat in the first seat by the

window. As the engine slipped into gear she mouthed, 'Lib-ra-ry,' and watched me, smiling, as the distance quickly lengthened between us.

ELEVEN

ALTHOUGH THE sun had been bright for several days there was still moisture in the soil. I rubbed some dirt in my fingers, cupped my hands over my nose. I breathed deeply. The smell made me think of my grandmother, the old clothes she had worn in the garden. Her hands were dry and had always smelled of the pig. It had lingered in her hair, and in the cap which still hung from the back of the door. It was in the soil, too. Grandad said he could taste it in the vegetables. Kneeling between two rows of turnips I took my grandmother's knife from my pocket. The blade was folded inside the handle, worn thin with sharpening and smoothed at the tip. Grandad's initials were carved into the handle. He had made the knife when he was younger, and in the conservatory there was a grinding wheel which he said he had pieced together from scrap.

It was just low enough to use from his wheelchair and sometimes when I called I had found him sharpening my grandmother's knives. It was one of the things he could do for her.

I sliced a small turnip in half and took it across to the sty. The pig lay on her side in the shade of the apple tree. Her back legs were straight and parted, her front trotters curled up to her body. When she saw me she grunted and quickly rose to her feet. I tossed the pieces of turnip into the pen and watched as she chased them, the first one to the wall, the other into a corner. She flopped down beside the smaller piece and crunched it in her teeth, her snout moist, starting to dribble. Even as she ate she continued to grunt. I leaned my elbows on the wall and looked back to the house. Some martins came and went from the roof. The downstairs windows reflected the garden, white and pink rosebushes, lengthening weeds.

There was a pack of my grandfather's cigarettes tucked into the belt of my trousers. I had found it between the cushions of his armchair when I was tidying the house, crushed into a wedge shape, already opened. As the pig began to eat the next piece of turnip I placed a cigarette in my mouth and walked back to the kitchen to light it. Bits of tobacco stuck to my tongue. He didn't use filter tips and his cigarettes tasted sour, made my mouth water. I spat into the drain under the kitchen window. It was full of vegetable peelings.

Indoors there was nothing more for me to do. After breakfast I had remained at the cottage, cleaning the cooker and washing the pots, wiping down all the surfaces. I had brushed out the conservatory and kitchen, hoovered the downstairs carpets. The machine had left balls of grey fluff in the bedroom and as I knelt to collect them I had found one of my grandmother's rings, a plain hoop of gold. It matched the pattern of circles in the rug on her side of the bed, dull yellow on red. I slipped it into the small pocket at the front of my jeans, but I did not remove anything else, the furniture remained in the same place, Gran's clutter of ornaments exactly as she had left it. I wanted Surinder to see the house as it always had been.

Bending to light my cigarette at the cooker I glanced at the clock and saw that it was my grandfather's lunchtime. I was already late. When I arrived I would give him his cigarettes and tell him I had been cleaning the house, pulling weeds from the allotment. I would not tell him why. Without locking the door I set off up the garden, taking short drags as I went. The pig was still chewing. I bolted the gate and ran down the hill to the dual carriage-way.

When I returned home after lunch our front door was open and the television flickering inside. Richard lay on the sofa watching a cricket match. With one arm he pillowed his head; his free hand trailed on the carpet. The blinds were drawn fast and the only sound in the room was the rhythmic beating of beer cans, a derisive cheering as the bowler ran in. I paused to watch the delivery, then walked through to the kitchen. 'Where've you been?' he shouted after me.

'Grandad's,' I said.

I filled the kettle to make tea, set two mugs on the worktop. Upstairs my father was snoring, a low grumble and then silence; another grumble. For several minutes I looked out at the garden. Mum's washing rippled on the clothes line, a faint breeze blew in the grass. When I was smaller I had tried to calculate how many times our garden would fit into my grandmother's allotment. I had measured it out in giant strides around the perimeter fence. It had made a neat square, twelve strides by twelve. At the time the discovery had seemed important and I ran upstairs to tell Mum. She was arguing with Dad but I thought my news would stop them. Before I could speak she had ushered me back to the landing and closed the door in front of me. I waited. Seconds later she started shouting again. For the rest of the morning I had paced the length of each room in the house, taking baby steps, the heel of one foot placed to the toe of the other. When my parents finally came from the bedroom they hadn't asked what I was doing, and I hadn't told them.

As the kettle began to boil Richard called from his sofa, 'Some guy from the Council came round.'

I dunked a teabag in each of the mugs and dropped it on the worktop. The milk spilled as I poured it. 'How come?' I shouted.

Richard looked up, and spoke through a yawn. 'Wanted to talk to Mum or something. About next door.'

I placed his mug on the carpet, next to his hand. 'Did he speak to Dad at all?'

'Didn't wake him.'

'Fuck's sake, Richard!'

He was about to throw me a cigarette, but paused and returned it to the packet. He lit his own, and said, 'Dad's asleep, Danny.'

Flecks of milk floated on my tea. I poked them with my fingertip. 'So what's happening?'

Richard gazed at the television. A ball rolled to the boundary beneath the camera, a fielder chasing it. The commentator sounded excited. The crowd began cheering. 'I've just told you,' he said finally. 'A guy from the Council came to see Mum.'

'About the bungalow?'

'Something like that.'

I sat forwards and watched him, the slow rise and fall of

his belly, his finger tapping ash from the cigarette. When the next ball crossed the boundary I said, 'So is he coming back at all?'

Richard shrugged. 'Probably. He didn't say.'

'Christ sake!'

The crowd applauded the batsmen, blew horns, and I pulled myself upright, crossed the room to the telephone. The receiver smelled of Mum's perfume. I searched the directory and found a page of Council departments, spoke the number aloud as I dialled. A woman's voice answered me, a short phrase in a clatter of typewriters. 'Sorry?' I said, and covered my other ear.

'Building and Works,' she repeated. She was laughing.

'Is Tom there?'

'I think you have the wrong department, love. This is Building and Works.'

'I'm looking for my brother-in-law,' I told her, and felt myself redden. I turned to the window. 'I thought that's where he worked. It's about a Council house.'

'Then you'll have to speak to Housing, love.'

'What number's that?' I looked down at the directory, scanned the names in bold type.

'Putting you through.'

The next phone began ringing before I could thank her, and at Housing it was a man's voice that spoke to me, an answering machine, careful and toneless. The pips began and I counted them, but I could not think what to say. As I put down the receiver I fumbled and it clattered onto the sideboard. Without glancing at Richard I went through to the kitchen. I picked up a dishcloth and dabbed at the puddle of milk on the worktop. Then I returned the carton to the fridge, wiped my hands on a tea-towel. I stood with my back to the sink. I could see Richard's feet through the doorway, a thick pair of grey socks. It was almost two o'clock. Soon he would get up to hoover the living room. It was what he did to help Mum. He pushed all the chairs to the wall and hoovered around them, then he lined the cushions in rows, diamond-shaped. He wouldn't do any more. As I left by the back door I heard him yawning aloud, the television suddenly silent.

TWELVE

I SAID, 'Richard called Tom a nobody.'
My sister allowed her hair to fall forwards and picked at a
thread in her lap. When she looked up she was facing the
French windows. 'That's Richard,' she said, smiling. She
balled the thread in her fingers and tucked it into the pouch
of her smock. She shook her head. Outside in the sun the girls
were drawing pictures. A sudden breeze lifted one edge of
Katie's paper and she tutted impatiently, waited until it lay
still. Before changing crayons she scolded the paper. She was
six years old and twice the age of Lucy, her sister, who was
lying face down beside her. They looked very alike. Their
hair was fine and cut short, faces rounded and pale. Lucy
was dressed in a frock the same style as her mother's. She
held a crayon in her fist, made circles on the back of a colour-
ing book. 'Would you like some juice?' Rachael asked me.

I nodded, watched as she went through to the kitchen. She walked with feet splayed, her ankles swollen above a pair of white plimsolls. I sat with my hands on my knees. Although her carpet was littered with toys, my sister's house never appeared to be cluttered, always smelled of fresh paint, clean washing. She kept flowers in vases, three shelves of books, but there were few other ornaments or pictures, no patterns on the wallpaper or furniture. My father always asked me when she was planning to move in.

When the girls heard the fridge door they abandoned their work and hurried in from the garden. I gazed through the front window at the neighbouring houses. I could re-member when the area was fields, common land where we came to find conkers, chase rabbits. There used to be a set of goalposts near the main road, swings tied to the branches of trees. My sister's estate had been built in less than a year, and the streets named after towns in Australia. If I mentioned them to Grandad his face became blank; he didn't know where they were, knew no people who lived there or stories about them. It was a place where the pavements always seemed to be empty. Every house had a garage, identical gardens enclosed by low walls, and some also had caravans, small boats under tarpaulins. On the next-door neighbour's lawn there was an estate agent's sign. It had been there since the previous summer.

'We've got juice, Uncle Danny.'

The girls came through from the kitchen, holding plastic cups to their lips, and Rachael followed with a glass of orange for me. The bulge of her stomach was round and smooth, her breasts heavy. The shape of her nipples and belly button showed clearly under her dress. As she gave me my drink she pushed the hair from her face and looked at me directly. 'I'm getting big,' she said, 'I know.' I felt my neck flushing red, held the glass to my cheek as she sat down. When I crossed my legs I noticed a smear of dirt on my heel.

'You not having one?' I said.

'Not just now.' She reached out an arm to straighten Katie's collar, and said, 'Show Uncle Danny what you've been drawing.'

Katie emptied her beaker and took her sister by the hand. She tugged her towards the French windows, speaking as a mother would do, explaining where they were going. I looked at my shoe. The dirt was pigshit. I said, 'Did Tom say he could get the flat then, Rachael?'

It was a moment before she replied, and she sighed as she spoke. 'He didn't say anything, Danny, but if someone's been round to yours then he's probably done all he can.' I nodded, and she added, 'You mustn't expect him to arrange it – it's not his job.'

I said, 'So what is his job?'

'Sales. You know what it is.'

'He works for the Council.'

Rachael smiled, and spoke as if to the ceiling. 'So do the road sweepers, Danny.'

As the girls returned to the room we turned to face them and Katie started to giggle, ran suddenly towards me. She slammed her pad on my lap and backed off to stand beside Rachael. Lucy did the same but stumbled, steadied herself by holding onto my foot. Some of the dirt came away on her hand. I placed both my feet on the ground and looked at Katie's drawing, a round shape with a curly tail, four legs in a line. 'He's nothing to do with letting properties,' my sister said then. 'He sells them. There's a difference.'

I said, 'I think Lucy's picked up some muck, Rachael.' And turning to Katie, I asked, 'What's it supposed to be?'

'It's a pig.' She placed her hands on her hips and took a big breath. 'What do you think it is!'

Rachael smiled at her, lifted Lucy's hand by the wrist. She frowned. 'This is shit,' she murmured, and looking at me she said, 'Danny, this is pig shit.' Her face was accusing. Lucy gazed at her dumbly.

'Are you sure?' I said.

'Yes, I'm sure.' She laboured to her feet, pulled Lucy across to the stairs. As I made to examine the soles of my shoes she said wearily, 'Just take them off, Danny,' and lifted Lucy to her hip.

I looked at Katie, who started to laugh. 'Pig shit!' she shouted, and grabbed for her pad as she ran back to the garden.

When I heard splashing water from the bathroom, Lucy chattering, I slipped my shoes from my feet and walked across to the bookshelves. After a moment I heard Rachael groaning. She crossed the landing above me, opened cupboards and drawers in a bedroom, slammed each of them shut. I looked along the spines of the books. They were mostly Tom's, detective stories and westerns, a few glossy hardbacks. There were packets of photographs too, pictures of the girls as babies, holiday snaps, and a white album of wedding photos. I had seen them before, but next to the telephone there was a small colour photograph of my grandparents. They were standing outside a caravan with Rachael and Richard. My brother was wearing blue shorts, Grandad laughing behind him. Gran was hiding a smile, her right arm around Rachael. On the back it said 'Grandma and Grandad' in my sister's best writing. It was dated before I was born.

When I was younger it was usually Rachael who had walked with me to visit my grandparents, but she rarely went on her own. Like my mother and father she often seemed uncomfortable in the tiny back room, and spoke too politely, with frequent glances at the clock on the fireplace.

For almost a year after her wedding she hadn't visited at all. She preferred to write letters, which my grandmother kept in a shoe box, though she was puzzled to receive them. And later, when Rachael began to visit in the car with Katie and Lucy, it was never for more than an hour at a time. They went every five or six weeks, and afterwards the girls spoke about seeing the pig, but hardly mentioned my grandparents.

As my sister began descending the stairs I quickly returned the photo to its shelf and craned my neck to read the titles of Tom's paperbacks. I held both my shoes in one hand. When she came through the door I reached for the photo again, and said casually, 'How come you've got this here, Rachael?'

She sent Lucy to play with her sister, came to take the photograph from my hand. As she sat down she said, 'It was in the drawer.'

'You should get it framed,' I said. 'It's starting to bend.'

Rachael flexed the paper, leaned over her stomach to place it on the mantelpiece. Resting her head on the chair-back she said, 'I could do I suppose.'

'I'll have it if you don't want it.'

'Don't you have enough already, Danny?' There was a tightness in her voice that took me by surprise, an edge of sarcasm or anger. I tried to smile but she looked away from me. She closed her eyes, took a deep breath. 'Have you spoken to Grandad about this bungalow, Danny?'

'What about it?'

'That he might not want to move there?'

I shrugged. 'He can't stay in the cottage, can he?'

'No, he wouldn't be able to cope on his own, Danny.' She spoke softly and carefully, as if to Lucy or Katie. 'So what makes you think he'll be able to live alone in the flat?'

'Us,' I told her. 'We'll be right next door.'

'Us?'

'Me. Richard. Mum and Dad.' Outside the girls had abandoned their drawings. Lucy was following her sister around the edge of the garden, pretending to water the plants.

'You think Richard is going to put himself out?' The girls stood perfectly still. There was something in the flower bed. 'Dad's on nights. Mum has enough on her plate as it is. And someone will have to do all his housework, all his cooking, all his washing. You don't realize how much work it is, Danny. Your gran was practically a slave to him.'

I walked towards the French windows. 'She wasn't a slave.'

'She was worn out, Danny. That's what killed her. Waiting on your Grandad, looking after that garden, that bloody pig. It was too much.'

'It was her pig,' I said. 'She wanted it. And the garden. She didn't do it for him.'

Rachael said quietly, 'She wasn't the kind to complain, Danny.'

My feet were soft on the carpet. I said nothing, stared out at the girls. Rachael waited for me. 'So where's he supposed to go?' I asked finally. 'He's only temporary in that Home.'

'He was taken in temporary,' she said. 'But if they've got room for him, which they obviously have, then they'll let him stay. Especially if they see he's got nowhere else to go. It's the best thing for him. He can be looked after properly, and he'll have all the company he needs.'

'Maybe,' I said. I stood outside, dropped my shoes on the ground. Katie was poking in the flowers with a plastic trowel, Lucy crouching beside her. 'What've you found?' I asked.

'Hedgehog,' said Katie.

'Mind you don't catch fleas.'

'It doesn't have fleas,' she told me, 'it has spikes.'

I tied my shoelaces, stepped onto the lawn. The fences were high all around us and the girls were in shadow. I knelt beside them. 'Show me,' I said, and leant on my elbows.

Rachael stood in the doorway behind us. 'Really, Danny. I just don't know what you're thinking of. You've got school to go back to, with any luck you'll get your exams and leave this place, do something with yourself. But you're dreaming. You've lumbered yourself with that pig, and the cottage, and now you want to look after your grandad as well.'

'Yeah,' I said. The hedgehog was balled tightly. Many of its spikes were broken, like the bristles on my grandmother's broom. I touched one, surprised at its bluntness. Katie took a step closer. 'It's an old one,' I whispered, and pointed to the spikes. 'Looks like it's been in the wars.'

'It's in a ball because it's hiding.'

'What is?' said Rachael.

'This hedgehog.'

'Right,' she said. 'You two. In here, now.' The girls hesitated, facing their mother. 'Now,' she repeated, and stood to one side as they ran past her.

I got to my feet. 'Fuck's sake, Rachael.'

She folded her arms. After a moment she said, 'All this time you spend at the cottage, Danny, have you thought through what happens when they realize there's no one living there?'

'Tell me.'

'They'll have the place knocked down. You know they will, and even if they don't they'll be wanting rent. Are you going to pay it?'

I shrugged. 'Don't worry about it,' I said.

'And the bills?'

I gazed at the bedroom windows next door. The net curtains were tied with blue ribbons. There was a satellite dish on the wall, a length of brown flex looped over the bracket. The roof guttering was plastic. I gazed at the houses which surrounded us, the empty windows upstairs, different curtains and blinds. The roofs had aerials, no chimneys. When Rachael sighed I didn't look at her. 'Are you coming or going?' she said. She was waiting, one foot on the living room carpet. She seemed to expect me to follow her.

I walked to the gate at the side of the house and drew back the latch. 'Going,' I said. 'See you later.'

THIRTEEN

A PACK OF Gran's cigarettes still lay on the window sill. I tossed them onto the table, then struck a match over the cooker. The gas popped and burned fiercely. 'Make yourself at home,' I said. Surinder draped her anorak over a chair, shivering as she sat down. She hugged her arms to her chest. Rainwater dripped from her hair. 'I'll fetch you a towel,' I said.

The kitchen and bathroom had once formed an outbuilding, standing at the end of the yard. Now the yard was completely enclosed and called a conservatory. Grandad had made the conversion before I was born, before the Council began our estate. He used whatever materials he found and constructed one wall from odd-sized panels of wood, surrounding a window. The other was brick. The sloping roof was corrugated iron. It was where Gran stored her tools and vegetables. A few onion strings hung from the beams, sacks of potatoes and pigmeal lined the brick wall. Everywhere the paintwork was peeling and when it rained puddles would form on the linoleum.

As she stood at her cooker Gran would be able to see into the conservatory through a single glass pane. Behind her the kitchen was dim-lit and spartan, all its surfaces topped with yellowing formica. There were no doors to the cupboards, just shelves stacked with crockery and cooking pots. A calendar was pinned next to the stove, spattered with fat and years out of date. She kept her wellingtons under the draining board. Her raincoat still hung from the back of the door.

Surinder sat with one arm on the table. The rain drummed on the roof of the conservatory, streamed down the window behind her. I slung the bathtowel over her shoulders and switched on the light. 'You're leaking,' I said. A puddle had formed round her sandals. She looked down, exhaling blue smoke.

'Any chance of some tea?' she said.

I lit another gas ring, filled up the kettle. Along one edge of the table there was a line of brown marks where Gran had put down her cigarettes. Surinder placed hers carefully beside them and pulled the towel over her head like a shawl. She parted her feet and bent forwards, rubbing her left ear. For a while I watched her, feeling the damp in my clothes. Then I turned and lifted a pot to the stove. The swill smelled of farts and I remembered how Gran would stir it around with her hand, peering over the rim. Sometimes she picked out a potato or carrot gone mouldy, perhaps a chicken bone. I took a long wooden spoon from a drawer, holding my breath.

'You said pigs will eat anything.'

'They do.'

Surinder flicked back her hair, smoothed it down with both hands. 'So why cook it?'

'Kills the germs.' I lowered the gas.

'It'll only get cold again.'

'It's meant to.' I concentrated on the swill, watching the bubbles. Surinder picked up her cigarette, inhaled and sighed deeply.

'What'll I do with this ash?'

I glanced round. 'Tip it in your hand.'

'My hand?'

'A saucer then.'

'Where?'

I stooped to retrieve a small plate from one of the shelves, but the ash fell before I could reach it. Surinder took another drag and I slid the plate on the table. 'What's up?' I said. She shook her head, blowing smoke from the side of her mouth.

'The kettle's boiling.'

We drank our tea without talking. When the cups were empty I rinsed them under a tap and left them to dry on the draining board. The pipes gurgled as the last of the water sank away. I leant back on the wall and folded my arms, crossed my legs at the ankle. Surinder opened the cigarette packet, looked inside and quietly closed it. When she began to hum I said, 'Shall I show you around then?' I pushed myself from the wall and waited, but she remained in the chair. 'Surinder?'

Slowly she turned round to face me, flicked the hair from her eyes. She was weeping. 'Come here first,' she said. I lowered myself to her lap and her arms closed round my waist. She rested her face on my chest. After some minutes she said, 'You smell of pig slops.'

'Sorry.' I shifted to make myself lighter, eased my hand round her shoulder. 'You smell of perfume.'

Surinder lifted her head, smiling at me. 'And your heart is beating like crazy,' she said.

The staircase was concealed behind a small door in the back room. It looked like a cupboard, as if the upstairs didn't exist. I lifted the latch and climbed the first step, ducking under the lintel. Surinder hesitated behind me. She pointed to the other door, beyond my grandmother's chair. 'What's through there?' she asked me.

I said, 'That's their bedroom,' and she nodded but didn't move. 'You can see if you like.'

She glanced at me, then back to the door. Her face wrinkled. 'Everything smells of old carpets, doesn't it?'

'Do you want to see?'

She shook her head. 'Later maybe,' and I let the door swing slowly behind us, taking the light. Surinder gripped my waistband. The stairs creaked as we climbed. There used to be a handrail but I couldn't find it, the wall was damp under my fingers. On the top landing I fumbled in the dark for the handles and pushed open both doors. We entered the largest room, at the front of the house, and I said, 'This used to be where Gran and Grandad slept, in the old days.'

It was unfurnished except for a wardrobe, too heavy to move even when empty. Surinder walked across the floor-boards to the window, drew a line through the dirt with a finger. She turned completely around, scanning the walls, as if there was anything to see. Then she stooped and peered outside. Softly she said, 'It's coming down buckets.'

'I can hear it.' Our voices mingled with the noise of the rain, echoing faintly.

'Poor rats,' she said. They were floating in a pail of rainwater outside. I had dug them from the compost heap, held them under the water with the blade of Gran's shovel.

Surinder had watched from a distance, didn't see what they looked like. She turned round. 'How will we get back?'

'Same way we got here.'

'But it's pouring.'

I said, 'There's some bikes through here.' She followed me into the back bedroom, where the bikes were resting against a small wardrobe. Their tyres were flat, the wheel-rims pockmarked with rust. Metal guards encased the chains, a thick coating of paint obscured any markings. The smaller of the two bikes had a basket. A brass horn was attached to the other. We took a couple of paces into the room and Surinder suddenly started. She clutched my arm. I glimpsed the movement in the mirror. She was staring back at me from the glass, her eyes wide, biting her lip. When she began to giggle I saw myself smiling.

I walked around the room. The furniture was heavy and dark, cluttered with trinkets and photos. I recognized most of the ornaments from downstairs, from when I was younger. There were clocks and stuffed animals, an ancient radio, brass figures and vases, some ashtrays from the seaside. The photographs were fading and speckled with mildew. Looking up I saw a row of caps and macs lining the back of the door. On one wall a barometer hung next to an old highland calendar, showing *Sunny* and *January*. This was where I used to sleep. Surinder sat on the bed and prodded the mattress. I bent over the bikes and squeezed the brake handles, pressed my thumb on the tyres.

'They're flat,' she said.

'I know. I was just seeing . . . I could fetch the slops in this basket.'

'You could do,' she said. She cupped her hands in her lap and watched me.

'In a tub,' I said.

'Or else it would spill out through the holes,' she said.

I edged back to the bed and sat down at her side. Our reflection was framed in the mirror opposite, familiar wall-paper behind us. I saw Surinder in profile, watching me, smiling. Her hand reached across my shoulder. She pulled me backwards. I could smell the rain in her hair, the musty scent of the bedclothes, old carpets. For a long time we lay in each other's arms, breathing heavily, not speaking. I watched the clouds shifting outside, the curtains rising and falling, caught in a draught. A wind gusted suddenly, rain spattered the window. When I was younger I had lain awake in this bed, listening to the steel works, the roar of the blast furnace, locomotives shunting over the points, metal tubes clanking in the sheds. Now Surinder whispered into my ear, 'Do you want to?' and pulling away I said, 'Yes.'

FOURTEEN

I COULD NOT remember my grandmother riding a bicycle. For most of my childhood the bikes were stored outside in a shed and concealed beneath a tarpaulin, never oiled or moved. When the shed collapsed in a storm I helped clear the wreckage to the edge of the garden. It was autumn and windy; wet leaves swirled around my ankles and tore from the trees. Several times I slipped in the mud. Whilst I tried to build a bonfire Gran took the bicycles indoors and carried them upstairs to the back bedroom. Later she brought down some photographs, a collection of tiny black and white snapshots. They had been taken before my mother was born and in one of them Gran was standing shoulder to shoulder with Grandad, small and dark in the sunshine and touching his hand. Their bicycles were propped against the gate of a churchyard and there were some flowers in my grandmother's basket. She was wearing a white bonnet which shaded her eyes; Grandad's trousers came up over his belly. They appeared to be smiling. Behind them a road sign pointed to somewhere called Sprowston.

A couple of weeks after Gran's funeral I found the photographs in an envelope at the back of the wardrobe. I slipped the packet in my shirt pocket and picked up her bicycle. I was going to bring it downstairs, perhaps take it outside. But it was not as light as I expected. The front wheel juddered from a wall and shook the whole frame; the left pedal struck my knee. As I came through the door at the foot of the stairs I left a scratch in the paintwork, exposing a layer of green beneath the yellowing topcoat. I set the bike down by the fireplace and searched through the photographs until I found the one I remembered. I placed it on the mantelpiece in front of the clock, then began work on pumping the tyres. It was several minutes before I realized that the valves should be loosened, and by the time the tyres were inflated my arms and shoulders were aching, my hands beginning to blister. I paused for breath, opened the tiny back window to let in some air. Later I attempted to adjust the height of the saddle but the nuts wouldn't budge; I found the gear cable had snapped and I didn't know how to fix it. But when I matched the swill tub to the basket I found they fitted exactly, and that was enough. I cycled out to see Grandad the next lunchtime. He was pleased that the bicycles were still in the house, and surprised that I had chosen to ride Gran's. The photographs, he told me, were taken on their honeymoon; the sun had shone all three days, and in Yarmouth they had made friends with some fish packers from Glasgow.

After feeding the pig that evening I rode the bicycle home. I left it propped against the paving slabs outside our back door and went to the supermarket. I bought a tin of bike oil, lowered my eyes as Mr Sidhu served me. I had not been to his shop since Surinder came to my grandparents' cottage. Marjory was removing her shop coat in the back room, preparing to leave. Mr Sidhu was just about to close up, the steel shutters already half-drawn. As I left through the passageway I heard them slam shut behind me and I started to run.

Under the stairs in our house my father kept a few tools in a biscuit tin, neatly folded in strips of grey canvas. I took them outside to the garden and turned the bicycle onto its saddle. I selected a spanner. As my mother watched from the kitchen window I tightened the brakes, dripped oil along the chain and over both axles, pumped more air into the tyres. The sun came low across the roofs of the buildings behind and reflected orange in our living room window. Richard appeared briefly inside. He parted the blinds with his fingertips, retreated from view when I saw him. Mum came to the doorway, folding her arms. 'You're working hard,' she said. I shrugged a shoulder, pressed the front tyre for firmness. 'Where did you find it?'

I twisted the pump from the valve. 'It was Gran's,' I said.

My mother watched me. I pushed the small rubber hose into the end of the handle, clipped the pump into the frame of the bike. I stood back to examine it, then turned to face her. My hands were greasy. 'They'll need scrubbing,' she said.

The scouring powder turned to grey along my arms, but the oil wouldn't shift from my fingernails. Mum gave me a nailbrush from under the sink, winced as she straightened. She pulled out a chair and sat at the table. She said, 'You've been spending a lot of time at the cottage, Danny.'

'Yes.'

She lit a cigarette, pulled the ashtray towards her. 'Is that where you were this tea-time?'

'All day,' I replied.

'What about food?'

'There's some out there,' I said. I rinsed my hands beneath the cold tap, looked out at the garden, the bicycle standing in shadow. 'Loads of it,' I added.

'Loads of it here too, Danny,' she said. 'Most of it in the bin.' I turned off the tap and dried my hands on the tea-towel. 'I cooked your tea,' she said. She held the cigarette a few inches from her lips, her elbow crooked on the table. When I met her gaze she lifted her chin and inhaled. Her cheeks were thin and made shadows. The sides of her mouth were drawn downwards. She was becoming old, I realized; her complexion was grey, and there was grey in her hair.

I said, 'There was no need to chuck it in the bin. The pig could still eat it.'

'The pig,' she said quietly. She nodded, stabbed her cigarette in the ashtray. After a moment she said, 'You're spending too much time out there, Danny. You shouldn't be around old people's things so much. That was your gran's house. I think it should be left alone now.'

I wiped my arms on the tea towel. 'What about Grandad?'

'He won't be going back there.'

'Someone has to look after the pig.'

'Someone doesn't,' she said, and rose to her feet. 'Someone has to look after your grandfather, but not the pig. No one has to look after the pig.'

During the following couple of days I rode the bicycle everywhere. I took it to the shops to fetch bread, pedalled around the streets of the neighbouring estates. In the town centre I bought a length of gear cable and a lock, nervously watching the concourse outside, the bicycle standing unguarded. Then I rode out to the country. I had no route in mind and passed several farms without stopping, turned left or right at junctions without reading the road signs. I saw no pigs, but several fields of sheep and cows, a few horses, some hedgehogs crushed in the road. It was hard work, the saddle was broad and chafed at my thighs, my legs soon became weary. At the first hill I came to I dismounted and pushed the bike to the top. Fields of green and brown stretched away on both sides. I saw several squares of yellow, a small lake, and on the horizon the blue and grey line of the town. I hadn't come this far before. I freewheeled down the next slope, leaning over the handlebars, watching the tarmac shooting beneath me. The wind flapped in my shirt and rattled the bicycle. When I reached the bottom I was standing out of the saddle and laughing, rolling towards a main road. The brakes barely made contact with the wheels and I had to put out my foot, bringing the bike to a halt several yards past the junction. There were no cars in either direction. I turned towards the town. As I cycled along the dual carriageway I decided I would repair my grandfather's bike too, and encourage Surinder to ride Gran's. We would come out together, perhaps look for Ted's farm, bring a picnic and some books to read in a field. They could fit into Gran's basket.

When I entered our kitchen my father said, 'That's coloureds moving in next door, Danny.'

He was making a cup of tea, stirring the bag around with a spoon. On the worktop beside him Mum had been preparing the dinner. There were carrots and scrapings on the chopping board, neatly cut potatoes in a saucepan of water. 'What?' I said.

'Ask your mother,' he said.

I looked round. She was standing in the living room, speaking into the telephone. Dad scooped out the tea bag and dropped it in the sink, tossed the spoon after it. He nodded in her direction as he went through the door.

I stood just inside the doorway. Sunlight sliced through the blinds and glazed the television screen. Mum flapped her hand, pointed at the set. I lowered the sound. 'I see,' she said then. 'Because I was told different, Tom.'

'What's he saying?' I asked, but she waved me to hush.

For several minutes she listened to Tom, and every few breaths she made a small noise through her nose. It might have been agreement or annoyance; her expression didn't alter. She stared out at the garden, one hand tucked under arm. When my brother came into the room she didn't look round. He crossed to the television and angled the set away from the window, turned up the volume.

Mum said, 'I'm not saying you personally, Tom, that's not what I meant.' She was frowning. The veins in her neck pulled when she spoke.

I leant my head on the wall, facing my brother and father. They sat close together, their legs outstretched and crossed at the ankle. Once they had seemed very alike, when Richard was at school and my father much younger. But now the resemblance was slight. Surinder said my brother looked like a pig and I told her his manners were worse. She said he was nearly as fat. Beside him my father appeared tired and frail, his clothes too loose, as if he had shrunk. His eyes were bleary from sleep. When Mum returned the phone to the sideboard he didn't look up from the television.

'That can't be right, can it?' she said. 'Dad's been in this town fifty-odd years, easily.'

'Fifty-seven,' I said.

My father cleared his throat, and said, 'You should make up your mind, Jean. Yesterday you didn't want him next door. He was better off in the Home with people paid to look after him.' He faced her then, and raised his eyebrows for confirmation. 'You were going to get onto the social worker about it because he wouldn't be able to cope on his own.'

Mum leant against the sideboard. She didn't reply and I said, 'So what's happening?'

Her eyes searched my face. Softly she told me, 'The Pakistanis are moving next door, Danny. Your grandad will have to stay put.'

'Which Pakistanis?'

'How do I know which ones? Does it matter which ones?' She sighed, ran a hand through her hair. 'I'd better get on with that dinner.'

'I peeled the spuds,' my father said. He sipped at his tea. Soon he would have to polish his shoes, start getting ready for work.

Mum hesitated, and said, 'There's no way I could look after Dad, is there? Not on top of everything else.'

My father shook his head. 'No, he's better off where he is. Next door's in no fit state anyway. There's only the pakis would take it.'

'Or Danny could move his pig in there,' Richard said. He narrowed his eyes, settled his chin on his chest. It was how my brother told jokes, not smiling, watching the television.

Mum said, 'I'd rather have neither.' Her face was anxious, still frowning. I gazed at the ceiling above me, the light-fitting, the lines in the plaster. My legs were aching, I could still feel the bicycle beneath me. Shaking my head, I turned into the kitchen and pushed the door closed behind me.

Beneath the sink there were detergents and aerosols, a

smell of dishcloths and polish. It was where Mum kept the swill bucket. I lifted it onto the worktop and prised off the lid. The vegetable knife was warm on the chopping board. As I raked the peelings into the bucket Mum came into the room and lit the gas ring beneath the potatoes. 'I'm sorry about that, Danny,' she said.

'About what?'

'Your grandad.'

I did not look at her, but opened the back door and went out to the garden. I took the swill bucket across to Gran's basket and wheeled the bike to the gate.

'What about your dinner?' she called.

'Don't bother,' I said.

FIFTEEN

OR A week or more the sun shone constantly. Each afternoon Surinder came out to the cottage to meet me and we went upstairs to the back bedroom. The sky was distant and cloudless, a perfect blue through the window, but inside the light barely penetrated. We lay on the bed surrounded by shadows and clutter, dusty mirrors, the lingering smell of my grandparents. The bed springs creaked with every movement and when we made love the frame rocked into the wall. Afterwards we spoke in near whispers.

Always when she arrived Surinder would be carrying a plastic bag from the library. She brought books about history and geography, old novels and plays, and made pencil notes in the margins, copied long passages into a spiral-bound notepad. Sometimes I lit a cigarette and watched her. More often I poked around in the bedroom, sipping cups of tea, looking in boxes and drawers.

One day I found a gardening guide on top of the wardrobe, in a metal box smelling of medicine. It was written during the war and coming loose from its covers. There was a fading V sign on the front. Dig For Victory! was printed at the top of each page. I sat on the mattress and flicked through the chapters, finding recipes and warnings, gardening advice for the beginner. I learnt that I mustn't allow a bonfire to burn after the blackout, that old soot on the leaves of celery and turnip will kill flies and beetles. The drawings all showed the same group of people, red-cheeked and healthy, their hair dark and shiny. They worked in checked shirts. Their gardens were leafy and tidy. I laid the book on the pillow and stared up at the window.

At the front of the house the grass was growing longer, sprouting dock leaves and dandelions, a few spindly thistles. Sometimes in the morning I tugged a handful of weeds from the allotment, left them to shrivel where they lay. Whilst the pig ate her meal I picked a way through the vegetables. The soil was damp and stuck to my heels. In the mist the leaves brushed against me and I remembered my grandmother, half-hidden in foliage, shaking the dirt from some onions. But although it was time, I did not begin to pull any vegetables, I could not decide where to start. Later in the day, when the stench from the sty became stronger, I remained indoors, repairing Gran's bicycle or lying upstairs with Surinder.

In the bedroom the air was stuffy and smelling of cigarettes. I gazed around at our shoes and clothes on the floor, ashtrays and mugs, an orange peel in a soup bowl. The pages of a newspaper were strewn in one corner. In the mirror I found our reflection, Surinder lying face down beside me. Her legs slowly kicked in the air. A pile of blankets had fallen to the foot of the bed and a tangle of sheets was drawn up to her back. When she looked round I said, 'Shall we move to the other room?'

'Why?' She closed her book and turned over to face me.

'It's gloomy in here.'

'It's gloomy everywhere,' she said.

'We'll get the sun in there.'

'And splinters in our bums.'

'We'll take the mattress.'

Surinder stood from the bed. She stretched out her arms. 'Okay,' she said, and watched as I dragged the mattress from the bedframe.

In the front room I had to force the window to open. I jabbed hard with the heel of my hand and it gave suddenly, a sharp crack. The sun's glare bounced back from the glass, illuminating the dark wood of the wardrobe. Specks of dirt sparkled like sand on the floorboards. I said, 'It's better though, isn't it?' Surinder stood in the doorway, a pair of shoes in each hand. Our trousers were draped over her arms and she held a book under each elbow. As she nudged the door closed she nodded and smiled. I smoothed my hand on the wallpaper. It was peeling away from the walls, a pattern of flowers and leaves.

'But do you know what it smells like?' she said.

'What?'

The books and shoes clattered on the floorboards as she dropped them. 'Carrots.' She flopped to the mattress.

'Is that bad?' I lay down at her side.

'It's okay.' She shrugged. 'Better than carpets anyway.'

I clasped my hands behind my head and for a long time I lay facing the ceiling. A patch of damp was spreading out from the window. Dirt clung to the light flex like a coating of fur and the bulb was unshaded, cloudy grey in the sunlight. I said, 'What's your favourite smell, Surinder?'

She yawned. 'The town centre library.' I waited. A wasp appeared at the window, ducked under the frame and disappeared from view.

'Is that it?'

'Bunches of coriander. Wet coriander.'

'And?'

She lowered herself on one elbow, swept her hair over her shoulder. 'Milky tea with cardamom pods.'

'And?'

She smiled at me. 'India.'

'What else?'

'That's loads,' she said. 'India's enormous.'

I said, 'Gran used to grow herbs and stuff. She picked them when the weather was like this, when they came into flower. I helped strip the leaves.' Surinder leaned across me. She examined my face, her eyes narrowed, biting her bottom lip. 'We used to tie them in bundles and hang them out in the conservatory, in the corner where it's dark, and then after a few weeks she took them down and we crumbled all the stalks and leaves onto newspapers. She packed them in these medicine jars and stored them away under the stairs. There should be some down there now.'

'Not coriander, though.'

'Probably not. There's mint and rosemary. All that stuff.'

'And you helped her?'

'Yes.'

She was grinning at me, showing her gums, and I said, 'What's wrong with that?'

'You're a hippy.'

'I'm not.'

She traced a pattern on my chest with her fingertips,

looking down, not at me. 'It's sweet,' she said. Her hair fell across her face. I could see that she was smiling, but when she looked up she said, 'This room's a bit bare though, isn't it?'

'It's okay,' I said, imitating her voice. Then, 'What else is sweet?'

Surinder reached across the floor for her jeans. She bunched the legs and slipped them quickly over her ankles. As she stood she made a small jump and pulled them to her hips. Before opening the door she said, 'I like your pink nipples.' Her footsteps were loud on the stairs and I listened as she went to the kitchen. I heard a pot or a jug being filled, the whine of water through the pipes. The back door shuddered as it opened. The pig began grunting from the top of the garden. I lay with my hands flat on my stomach and peered along the length of my body. I curled my toes, balanced one foot on top of the other. Steepling my fingers together I examined the dirt in my thumbnails. Then I looked inside my T-shirt, the faint elevations of my nipples, a few wisps of pale hair between them.

Surinder's sandals lay by the side of the mattress and when she returned to the bedroom her feet were dusty with soil. She had brought a glass vase from the kitchen, a large clump of flowers and weeds from Gran's garden. She sat heavily beside me, still panting from the stairs, and placed the flowers on the mattress. As I rolled onto my side she said, 'I broke the stems with my nails.' She had picked two of everything. I spread the stalks on the floor and arranged them in order of size. We took turns at choosing, standing them up in the vase. The heads of the largest flowers flopped over, the smallest sank into the water.

I said, 'My brother's got really big nipples, you know. He's almost got tits.'

Surinder removed two long stems from the vase. She slid

them back, closer to the middle. Pulling the flowers into shape she said, 'He comes in the shop, but I can never make out what he's supposed to be saying. He grunts.'

I gathered the stripped leaves and took them to the window. As I parted my hands I said, 'He's ignorant.' The leaves fell as a clump to the garden.

'He's shy,' Surinder said. She held up the vase, turning it slowly. 'He never looks at you. He always seems really embarrassed, pink all over.'

'That must be someone else.'

'No, its definitely him. I've seen him sitting on your doorstep when I go home. In his slippers, and his Union Jack T-shirt.'

'He doesn't have a Union Jack T-shirt.'

Surinder placed the vase on the floor at the head of the mattress. She sat with her knees drawn up, wrapped inside her arms. She stared at the flowers. 'I must've imagined it then.'

I lay down on my belly and rested my chin in my hands. Finally I said, 'Most of these are weeds.'

Her eyes turned towards me. 'Most of the garden is weeds,' she said.

'We ought to do something about it.'

'Tomorrow,' she said.

SIXTEEN

IT WAS another bright afternoon. As we came from the house I caught a warm breath of pig dung, and something sharper, carried on the breeze. A few gulls circled over the railway cutting, sweeping down to the tip, out again into sunshine. The quarries shimmered beyond them. I rolled up my sleeves and leant against the sty wall. The pig was hiding in her shelter, came out in a tumble of straw, mud-spattered and grunting. Her feet clacked across the hard ground.

Surinder said, 'I always thought they were pink, you know, like sausages. I can't believe she's so hairy.'

'She's turning grey,' I said. I held out my hand and the pig scrabbled upright, pressing her snout to my palm.

'She is grey,' Surinder said.

'White then.' A gust of wind blew from the quarries. I could taste it. 'She stinks too,' I said.

'It's not that bad. I quite like it.'

I raised my eyebrows.

'Honestly,' she said.

'You'll take it home with you.'

'Doubt it.' Her fingernails rasped as she scratched the animal's throat. She was wearing Gran's raincoat and wellingtons, her hair pinned beneath a check cap. I'd watched her undress in the kitchen, in the sunlight. 'Not in this get-up,' she said.

'You'd be surprised,' I told her. 'It gets right in the pores of your skin, lingers for days. We'll probably have to get in the bath.'

'We?'

'Plenty of soap,' I said. Surinder smiled but didn't look at me. Then the colour began to rise in her cheeks and I said, 'Scratch behind her ears, see if she's got lice.'

'Where!' She pulled her hand away, stepped backwards.

The pig snorted and dropped down on all fours. She edged across to her trough, into the shade. 'I only meant maybe,' I said.

We walked around the edge of the sty. Thick clumps of weeds sprouted from the base of the wall and I saw a stick, the end of a broom handle, propped against it. As the pig waited beneath me, her ears and tail pricked, I combed the handle back through her bristles, watching for movement. Surinder rested her chin in her hands. 'Well?' she said.

'I don't think she has any,' I said.

'I just saw one.'

I looked hard, raised myself on tip toe. 'Show me.'

'Two,' she said, and pulled the cap from her head. 'If you think I'm going in there . . .'

But I was already walking, and called over my shoulder,

'It's okay, Gran keeps this bottle, works every time. I've seen her.' Surinder looked at me doubtfully, folded the cap into her pocket. 'We'll need the wheelbarrow anyway,' I shouted.

In the dry air of the greenhouse everything was dying. Gran's tomato plants were yellow and straggly, lurching over on the weight of a few hard green fruit. Rows of seed trays held only soil. I picked up a margarine tub and tapped it on the edge of a bench. The soil came away in a block, fell apart in my fingers. Beneath the bench there was a watering can, some weed-killer and fertilizer. As I knelt down I saw the bottle lying on its side in a corner. It was half full of brown oil, smeared with grease and grimy to touch. The label said Lemonade. Looking closely I could see the imprint of my grandmother's fingers.

Surinder stood in the doorway and I said, 'The cap's screwed on too tightly.' A strand of hair fell over her face. She blew it away and gazed around at the trays.

'Shouldn't you water this lot?'

'I think they've had it,' I said. 'We're too late.'

I pulled a dead shoot from a pot and tossed it to one side. Surinder touched the handles of Gran's tools. 'Shall I take a spade then?' she said.

'If you like.' I gave her the bottle. 'And this.'

The wheelbarrow clanked across the hard ground and made my arms shudder. It was difficult to steer and pulled to the right, almost tipped over when I tried to turn left. The pig's face appeared and disappeared above the sty wall. When I whistled she gave out a screech, then became very quiet. At the gate I paused for Surinder. The pig was ready to bolt, standing quite still, and as I drew back the latch I whispered, 'Don't let her escape,' and pushed through with my hip. I pulled the barrow after me. Surinder stepped into the gap and stood close behind me.

'Poor old Agnes,' she said.

'Agnes?' The gate rattled on its hinges as I closed it. The pig returned to her shelter.

'You should let her get out sometimes.'

'She does get out.'

Lying on her side in her hut the pig seemed much longer and larger. I had to duck to get in beside her. Surinder crouched with me. 'Like when?' she asked me.

'Why's it important?' I twisted the cap from the bottle and poured the oil in a line down the pig's spine, over and round both ears, rubbing it in with one hand. I could remember watching as Gran performed the same job, her back rounded towards me, her hands working briskly. She rarely took the time to explain things, or even to talk, and I couldn't be sure if I was doing it right. As quickly as I moistened my hands they dried in the pig's bristles.

Surinder said, 'Well how would you like to be locked away all day, with no friends, nothing to do, nothing to look forward to?'

'But I'm not a pig,' I replied. I lay the empty bottle on its side and slapped the animal hard on her rump. As she skipped into life her heel struck my knee, a sharp crack. I fell backwards. Surinder tried to help me but I waved her away. I could barely stand.

'Serves you right,' she said, smiling.

With my teeth clenched I limped across to the wall which faced the allotment. A butterfly drifted over Gran's onions, vanished in the shade of the rhubarb. The bulbs showed as silvery globes in the soil and long flowering stems curved out from their leaves. Other vegetables stretched back in rows to the house, carrots and cabbages and sprouts, all laid in the spring and now overgrown. I shielded my eyes and looked beyond the greenhouse to the bean trellis. It was obscured by thick foliage, surrounded by nettles.

'If you let her out,' Surinder said then, 'she might eat up some of those weeds.'

'Very witty,' I said.

The pig's dung lay banked against the opposite wall, seeping yellow to the centre of the sty. When Surinder took up the spade I returned to the greenhouse for a fork. I started in on the onions, loosening the earth, tugging hard from the base of the stems. There were dock leaves and chickweed, a few scrawny thistles, and I pulled these up too, laying them in a line alongside the onions. I made a neat job and it wasn't until I reached the end of the row that I heard Surinder's spade on the concrete, a persistent chisel-like scraping. The noise had been there all along, and as I went closer I saw that she was chipping at dried slithers, determined to dislodge them.

'What about that pile by the wall?'

'I'm getting these first,' she said.

'But they've been there for years, it's a waste of energy.'

'My energy.'

'It's pointless though.'

Surinder sighed; her mouth tightened. She walked abruptly to the far wall and thrust her spade deep into the dung. As she crossed to the wheelbarrow a large lump fell from the blade and she went back to retrieve it, using the toe of her boot, growing angry. I walked around to the gate. 'Shall I do it?' I asked.

'I can do it myself.'

'But you should bring the barrow to the dung, you're doing it all wrong.'

She spoke to the dungheap. 'So who's watching?'

As she lifted the next load I said, 'I am.'

'Then go and dig some more weeds.'

'They were onions,' I said. I remained where I was standing but Surinder ignored me. For several minutes longer she continued to carry the muck in spadefuls across the length of the sty. When finally she wheeled the barrow to the pile I saw the flicker of a smile. She loosened her hair and allowed it to cover her face. 'I'll make us some tea,' I said, but she didn't answer me.

Surinder's clothes lay in a heap on the kitchen table, her sandals beside them. Whilst the tea brewed I picked up each garment and folded it carefully. Then I gripped the mugs in one hand and took a stiff brush in the other. I was whistling as I came around the side of the house. I didn't see the pig until I was almost upon her. The tea spilled and scalded my fingers. As I bent to put the mugs on the ground she took a hurried step backwards, and another, twitching her snout at my scent. Her eyes were like blind dots in the sunshine. Grandad once told me they saw the world through their nostrils, if you hammered a pig on the head its brains would come out through its nose. Gran said their eyesight was perfect, they could see the wind blowing. I sucked on my fingers, and Surinder smiled from the sty. 'What did you let her out for?' I shouted. Her smile broadened. The pig scurried away through the allotment, came to rest by the brussels, squealing and burping. There was no point in chasing her.

'You spilled half my tea,' said Surinder.

'She'll wreck the garden,' I said.

'You don't know.'

We watched as the pig rooted along a row of potatoes. She was excited and nervous, unable to settle. Twice she lifted her head as if suddenly alarmed, tensing her muscles and listening for movement. Then suddenly she bolted through the apple trees, hiding herself in a patch of long grass. A few seconds later she trotted into the open, her nose to the ground. Surinder began to sweep the floor of the sty. I emptied the dregs from my mug and dropped the cigarette butt under my foot. Stacked inside the pig's shelter were three bales of fresh straw, the last of more than a dozen. I ducked into the darkness and kicked away the old bedding, raked down a new bale with the fork, spreading it around me. Surinder piled the soiled straw on top of the dung, and as I heaved the wheelbarrow from the sty the pig gave out a shriek from the trees, came charging back through the allotment.

In the corner of the garden farthest from the house I tipped the barrow onto its side and began to mix the dung with the straw, piling it onto the remains of Gran's compost heap. On the other side of the railway cutting a solitary gull sat perched on the edge of the *LeisureLand* hoarding. From this distance I could see the blisters in the paintwork, green patches of fungus above the lettering. The air was heavy with the stench of the tip, teeming with insects. When I paused from rebuilding the compost I glimpsed Surinder walking backwards through the allotment. I wiped the sweat from my face and watched her. She was holding a mixing bowl, throwing down a trail of pig nuts. The animal followed at a couple of yards, and when it paused Surinder paused too, gently coaxing it to continue, all the way back to the sty. She closed the latch on the gate and brushed her hands down the sleeves of Gran's raincoat, looking at me, her chin raised and smiling. I clapped my hands and she curtsied, arms wide to each side.

SEVENTEEN

THE BATHROOM was small and without natural light. A single bulb glowed from a bracket nailed over the door. The walls and ceiling were speckled with damp and the paintwork was yellow, in places brown, the way that teeth go. When I turned on the taps the water came out in spurts, a reddish orange at first, running to pink as the steam started to rise. The geyser thrummed like a small engine, began to knock as its casing expanded. There was a rubber mat draped over the side of the tub, a steel handrail attached to one wall. I dropped the mat on the floor and quickly undressed, turning away from Surinder. She unbuttoned Gran's raincoat, let it fall from her shoulders and folded it neatly. She was naked except for her pants and a bangle.

As the bath filled I swept my hand through the water.

Without my clothes I felt a need to make lots of noise and I gasped loudly when I climbed in, louder still as I sat down. Surinder stood with one arm crossed over her stomach, her other hand touching her collar bone. I drew in my legs to make room and without looking at me she eased herself into the water, sinking back until it lapped to her chin. Her breasts buoyed outwards. She closed her eyes and leant her head between the taps.

'Are you comfortable?' I asked.

'No.' She placed one foot flat on my chest. Just under my chin there was a triangle of sunburn, freckles down my forearms. The fine black hairs on her shins were flattened in waves by the wet. I began soaping the water, making it cloudy, and she said, 'Did your gran and grandad have baths together?'

'Be a tight fit if they did.'

'When they were younger.'

'They used to fill a bath in front of the fire in the living room, but that was too small. They took turns.' I smoothed the soap down her leg and around the back of her knee. She curled her toes on my sunburn. As I worked the soap to a lather I said, 'It's hard to imagine them being younger. It's like they were always old, and Grandad's always been in a wheelchair. He built this bathroom you know.'

'It was very good of him.'

She offered her other leg and sank a little lower in the water, holding onto the sides of the bath. There were hairs under her arms, thicker than mine. She gazed at the cabinet over the sink. The mirror was misted with steam. A single red toothbrush sat in a glass beaker, its bristles discoloured and flattened with use. I said, 'That was my gran's, she kept it for years.'

'Did she polish her boots with it?'

'Just her teeth.' I cleaned carefully between each of her

toes. My hand was broad and red-knuckled, her foot pale, the width of three fingers. I pressed my palm to her sole and measured its length. 'Your feet are tiny,' I said.

'No, you've got bit mitts. Why didn't she get herself a new toothbrush?'

'She only had five teeth left, and they were practically rotten anyway. She used to press her lips together when she smiled, and she'd hardly open her mouth when she was speaking to you. She was self-conscious about it. Grandad kept telling her to get false ones. He kept saying her breath smelled.' Surinder widened her eyes, and I said, 'He's not that bad. You should come and meet him – tell him how much you enjoyed his bathroom.'

'What makes you think I'm enjoying it?' She swept her fingers through the water. 'Lying around in a tub of dirty water? With you? Clean people take showers.' I pinched her big toe, and she said, 'Does he even know about me?'

'He has an idea,' I said.

'But you haven't actually told him?'

'It's embarrassing.'

'What is?'

'Saying, I've got a girlfriend, Grandad.'

'And she's a Paki.'

'That's not what I meant.' I dropped the soap, felt it slip through my fingers. 'He wouldn't mind about that anyway,' I said.

Surinder drew herself up by her elbows and twisted around until she was kneeling. The water rose to the rim of the bath, splashed back over her hips and onto the floor. She had the soap in one hand. As she knelt over me she said, 'But that's how they think, Danny.'

'Not all of them.'

She raised her eyebrows, her head inclined to one side. She didn't look at my face, and as she worked the soap in her hands I gazed at her breasts. 'He's never mentioned anything to me anyway,' I said. 'And he usually says whatever comes into his head. I don't think he thinks about things like that.' She moved a little closer, began to spread the soap over my shoulders, around the back of my neck. I said, 'I don't think he really follows what's going on in the world. He lives in the past.'

Surinder dabbed some soap on my nose with her thumb. 'And you want to live in the past with him.' She leaned across me, placed the remains of the soap on the edge of the tub. Then she sat back on her heels, her hands in her lap. 'I can just see you – some grouchy old man in a cap and a grotty brown cardigan, packet of fags, pot of tea, pig outside in the garden.' She scooped a handful of water over my chest, washed down the soap suds. I cupped a hand over her breast and held it, and when she didn't prevent me I reached for the other, feeling their weight, the hardening whorl of her nipples against me. Softly I pressed upwards, turning my palms outwards. Her nipples appeared at the base of my thumbs, and when I drew my fingers around them she touched the back of my hands, turning her head to look down.

Quietly I said, 'You know when we find Gran's farmer, we could ask him about breeding the pig.'

Surinder's eyes met mine, half-smiling, and gently she lowered my hands to the water. 'Our own little family of piggies? What would we do with them, Danny?'

I reached forwards, patted her belly. 'Fatten them up!'

'You're joking. Can you imagine it?' I shrugged. She counted out on her fingers. 'They'd all want to be fed at the same time – so you'd have to make more swill for a start. They'd all be squealing at the same time and they'd all be shitting at the same time. Agnes would go right round the bend, and,' she plunged her hand between my legs and tickled me, 'they'd all end up as sausages in Sainsbury's or somewhere.'

'But it'd be good for Agnes,' I said. 'It'd be company for her.'

Surinder raised herself to a crouching position and sank backwards. She straightened her legs to either side of me. The bathwater lapped lukewarm against my chest and I slipped my feet under her buttocks, rested my hands on the edge of the bath. She said, 'But the babies would just get sliced up and turned into someone's breakfast, Danny. They'd be made into bacon and my dad would probably sell them to your mum, and she'd cook them for your brother, and then he'd get even fatter.'

'That's okay,' I said. 'It's natural. People have to eat.'

'But baby pigs?' she said.

I held her ankles under my arms, hugged them close to my ribs. 'And if the first litter is successful,' I said, 'we could maybe even start up our own pig farm, and you could be the farmer's wife.'

She dug her toes in my back. 'And who'd be the farmer? You, I suppose? No way.'

'Why not?'

'Farmers are fascists who kill baby pigs.' She leaned forwards and prodded my belly, her breasts dipping in the water. 'Our baby pigs. Besides which, you told me Agnes is ancient. It'd probably kill her.'

'Maybe,' I said. Then, 'I suppose so.' Surinder lay with her head between the taps. In the silence I heard a noise like the door of car, but when I listened closely there was only the hum of the fridge in the kitchen, my own breathing, a hollow drip from the water tank behind us. The air in the bathroom had cleared and the bathwater was cloudy, cold when I moved. I gazed at our clothes on the floor, my grandmother's toothbrush, the streaked glass of the mirror above it. When I looked at Surinder she was smiling. I said, 'Shall we have sex?'

'Danny!' She slapped the water with the back of her hand, splashing my face. I lifted my arms, about to retaliate, but then she pulled the plug by its chain. I hesitated. She bent her knees to stand up, and splashed me again. 'Only if you promise to build me a fire,' she said.

'Where?' The water was in my mouth, tepid and tasting of soap, faintly metallic.

'In the living room.'

I spat in my palm and dipped it under the surface. 'It's the middle of summer,' I said.

'My hair's wet.'

'You can dry it outside in the sun.' I stood with her. She placed her hands on my bottom, pressing against me. I closed my arms around her and squeezed. The bath emptied quickly, the water sucking at my ankles as she kissed me. There was a clacking sound in the pipes like a labouring engine, a final gurgle from the plughole. Surinder giggled, and stopped suddenly as my brother shouted my name from the kitchen.

EIGHTEEN

A FEW DAYS after my grandfather was taken into the Home my mother had come out to the cottage and hoovered and dusted his bedroom. She half-closed the curtains and stripped down his bed, reset the ornaments and polished the mirrors. She bundled Gran's slippers and nightclothes into a binbag. She hadn't asked me to help her and soon afterwards the dust had settled again. A smell of mothballs and hair oil remained. From time to time I came and stood by the window, enjoying the half-light, the stillness and quiet. But Surinder wouldn't come into the room, she didn't want to see where my grandmother died. Gran's chair still sat next to the sideboard. The varnish had worn from the armrests and the cushions were threadbare. Wherever I stood in the room I was aware of its being there. When I left I would glance at it quickly and pull the door fast behind me.

As I came now from the bathroom, still drying my hair in a towel, I saw my brother bending down at the sideboard. He was holding open both doors and peering inside. When he heard me he straightened. Sweat glistened on his forehead, wide patches of damp spread out from under his arms. I said, 'What are you doing here?' and he smiled because I was angry. He held out his hand for the towel and dabbed at the back of his neck, along the line of his jaw.

'Just thought I'd take a look,' he said. 'See what you get up to.' His voice was hoarse and he started to cough. I leant on the door, pressing until I heard the latch click. Richard patted himself on the chest as he coughed. Although his complexion had darkened the rims of his eyes and his nostrils were pale. He breathed through his mouth.

I said, 'You look a bit hot and bothered.'

'Yeah.' He tossed me the towel, tapped his fingers on the edge of the sideboard. He looked down at the clutter of vases and ashtrays. There was a watch which had stopped when we were children, a small black alarm clock and several framed pictures. Grandad's cough sweets sat in a fruit bowl. 'It's this weather,' he said. 'I don't feel too good.' He took a sweet from the bowl and reached across for a photograph. It showed himself aged about five, standing in the garden in summer. Despite the sunshine he was dressed in a quilted blue anorak and the hood was tied up, shielding his eyes. 'That's probably the last time I was out here,' he said. 'It's not changed much. Same curtains, all this lot.' He blew at the dust on the picture frame. 'Same dirt anyway.' The sweet clacked against his teeth. There was a creak on the stairs.

'The dirt's new,' I said quickly. 'Gran kept the place clean, it was spotless. I haven't been dusting because there's too much work with the pig.' My brother looked at my hand on the doorknob. I loosened my grip. 'I've just been mucking her out, that's why I was in the bath.'

'If you say so,' he said. He turned towards his reflection on the far wall, a round mirror in a wrought-iron surround. The mirror was convex and made his face curve outwards. He thrust his chin forward, touching his stubble. 'This glass could do with a wipe too, Danny. Reckon you'll get around to it?'

'Don't know,' I said.

'Think you ought to,' he said. He pulled open the doors of Gran's wardrobe and I watched as he ran his hand along a rail of her frocks. They were mostly patterned with flowers, like curtains or chair covers. He looked beneath them. 'Didn't Joe keep a bottle in here somewhere?'

'He kept it in the sideboard.' A suede boot fell onto its side. It was lined with white fur and the zipper was open. 'You're messing Gran's things,' I said.

'Yeah, sorry.' He righted the boot and pushed the door closed. I stiffened. There was a movement upstairs. Richard glanced over his shoulder. 'So where's it hidden?' he said.

'What?'

'The bottle.'

'You're too late,' I told him. 'Grandad asked me to take it across.'

'Right.' He nodded, felt in each of his pockets for cigarettes. He drew out a packet of ten.

I said, 'Is that why you've come here, looking for booze?'

'No, mate, nothing like that.' He dragged an ashtray across the sideboard, lowered himself into my grandmother's chair. He gazed around at the room. 'It's a nice little set-up you've got here, Danny. I reckon I might come and join you. We could make a go of this pig-breeding lark. What do you reckon?' He held the packet between his forefinger and thumb. I shook my head and he tossed the pack on the bed. 'Have them later,' he said. He stretched out his legs. 'You're well off here, Danny seriously, you're well out of it. Mum's a basket case, she nips your ear about everything – if it's not the hoovering it's this lot moving next door, she never stops moaning. Everything's a crisis.' He tapped some ash in the ashtray, rubbed one eye with his knuckle. 'And it's not like the pakis are even a problem,' he said. 'If we don't want them we don't have them. Simple.' He took a long drag from the cigarette and leaned his head on the back of the chair. As the smoke curled from his nose he lowered his eyelids.

'How?' I said.

'What?'

'How do you stop them, the Asians, if they have a right to be there?'

My brother smiled but he did not open his eyes. He repeated 'the Asians', and gave a faint shrug. 'You just make sure they don't feel welcome, Danny.' His smile faded slowly and I watched as his cigarette burned down to its stub, listening for movement upstairs. The only sound in the room was his breathing. When finally he started to snore I poked his leg with my toe. 'That's the chair Gran died in,' I told him.

In the kitchen Richard splashed cold water on the back of his neck. He cupped the water in his hands and held it over his face, gasped as he shook himself dry. I filled a kettle from the tap he left running, dropped a teabag in each of three mugs. My brother cleared his throat. 'One for the pig, Danny?' he said.

'What?' He nodded at the mugs and I felt myself redden.

'I do that sometimes. I used to make tea for Gran and Grandad.'

'Right,' he murmured, and watched as I returned the teabag to its caddy. I closed the door on the conservatory. Richard walked around the kitchen, looking at things, touching them. He lifted the lid from the swill pot, narrowed his eyes as he smelled it. 'What is it, Danny? Soup?'

'Pig swill,' I said.

'Yeah?' He grimaced, and said quietly, 'Stinks like fuck anyway.' He opened the back door and spat at the concrete. Breathing deeply he stepped outside. I hung Surinder's cup on a hook and watched as Richard walked around to the side of the house. The shadow of a cloud passed over the steel site. Moments later I heard him choking, being sick in the garden. I sat down at the table and waited for the water to boil.

When I gave him his tea he took it without looking up. He was sitting on the rubbish bin, bent forwards and sweating. 'You okay?' I said.

'I will be, mate.' He hacked up some phlegm and spat in the grass. 'In a minute.'

'Have you been drinking?'

'No, Danny. Not since Saturday.' He looked up to the sky. A house martin appeared from the roof guttering, flew over our heads to the garden. 'It's probably this sun, Danny,' he said. 'The weather or something, I dunno.'

I nodded. Flies had begun to gather where he'd been sick and his shoes were spattered. The trousers he wore belonged to his suit, and his shirt had come loose at the back. I wondered what had happened to his jacket and tie. 'How come you're out here?' I asked.

He tugged at his nose, suppressing a smile. 'Been for a job interview,' he said.

'Where?'

'Across the way, two guys in a Nissen hut.' He blew on his tea. 'Start a week tomorrow,' he said.

'Doing what?'

'Dunno.' He shrugged. 'Labouring or something. They're building a theme park, Danny.'

'That's good,' I said.

He held my gaze, and looked down, shaking his head. 'Not really, mate. It's peanuts.' He drew a long sigh and stood up, tilted his mug at the garden. 'I was looking at this earlier,' he said. 'It's some plot.' We walked a short distance along the gravel path, stopped beside a patch of rhubarb. I wanted to keep walking, away from the house, but Richard remained where he was standing. He stared at the vegetables. 'How long did they live out here, Danny?'

'Fifty-seven years.' I said. I glanced at the upstairs window. There was nothing to see.

'Amazing how it keeps going.'

'Pigshit,' I said.

'Yeah.' He drained his tea in one gulp and passed me the mug. 'If you're lucky,' he said, 'I might get to knock off early, maybe come over and help you. What do you say? Make it a going concern – little cottage garden, bacon factory up there, you do all the work and I'll sign the cheques. How about it?'

I pursed my lips, as if giving it some thought, but I avoided meeting his smile. He continued to watch me. I tore away a piece of rhubarb leaf and rolled it between my hands. 'These shallots could probably come out now,' I said, pointing. 'I meant to do it earlier. You see how they go all yellow and droopy?' I began to walk towards the sty and Richard followed, his hands in his pockets. 'The leeks need thinning as well,' I told him. 'You could do some now if you like.'

My brother shook his head. 'Like I said Danny, I'll leave

the grafting to you. Just pass me the notes when we're in profit.'

I said, 'You might as well help since you're here, there's plenty needs doing.'

'Danny, behave! You saw me, I was puking two minutes ago.' He shook his head and I said nothing more. The pig snorted from her sty. A small yellow-breasted bird settled on the roof of the shelter and Richard looked at it closely. Once, when I was five or six years old, he had allowed me to follow him into the country to find birds' eggs. He had a collection at home, kept under cotton wool in a shoe box and pierced with a pin at both ends. Some schoolfriends were supposed to meet him but we waited for nearly an hour and they didn't turn up. In the woods we found the nests of blackbirds and thrushes, saw several pigeons' too high to reach, and came home with nothing. It was the last time he went, and soon after he gave his eggs to a jumble sale. In his bedroom at home he still kept a bird-spotter's guide. It was the only book he owned, and I knew if I asked him he would be able to identify the bird on the shelter. Instead I stayed silent. I looked down at the cups I was holding, gently chinked them together, and waited for him to leave.

Finally he said, 'I met Craig the other night, Danny. He's got family in the meat business, reckons he could help you out if you're interested.'

His voice was cautious. I said, 'Who's Craig?'

'You met him. He's a mate of mine, runs a red transit.'

I shrugged. 'Don't remember,' I said.

Richard nodded. 'Well the offer's there, Danny. That pig won't last forever. It's worth thinking about.'

'I'm not interested,' I told him.

'No,' he said, and patted his trouser pockets. 'Where's my fags anyway?'

'You gave them to me, they're in the house.'

'I fancied one to smoke down the road.'

'You can have them back. I'll fetch them.'

'No, forget it. You keep them.' He hesitated, looking across my shoulder to the cottage. His face was pale but there were blotches of red on his forehead. His eyes were bloodshot, barely focused. He smiled to himself and patted my arm as he turned for the gate. 'I'll maybe catch you later,' he said. He was still smiling as he fastened the latch, but he didn't look back. I watched until he disappeared from view, until Surinder came out from the house to stand with me.

NINETEEN

THE WHISKY burned in my throat, my eyes misted. I tipped what remained of my glass into Grandad's and sat back to wait for him. He was in the lavatory across the corridor. When he pulled the chain a surge of noise ran through the pipes to his bedroom, then the toilet door clicked open. A woman's voice called out from the end of the corridor.

Grandad replied, 'Aye, what it is, Janet?'

Her footsteps padded closer, the voice talking but making no sense. I gazed around his room, at the smooth bare walls, blue linoleum, fitted wardrobe and sink. He had brought no pictures or ornaments. Lying in the shadows beneath his bed I could see his false leg, a spare boot and a bedpan. I looked out of the window.

The graveyard was quiet. An old lady in a raincoat and

boots was walking towards the exit, her head bowed, carrying a trowel. A jar of yellow flowers moved on a breeze as she passed them, a bird hopped from shadow into sunlight. The woman looked like my grandmother, but taller.

'Aye,' said Grandad then. 'Okay, Janet. Aye.' He bumped the door with his chair and wheeled himself into the room. I watched as Janet hesitated behind him, about to speak again. She squeezed her hands together, looked at me, then turned suddenly away. She was wearing her dressing gown and her hair was uncombed. Grandad pushed the door shut.

'Mrs Speakaminute, son. She hasn't a clue, she's away with the fairies.' He manoeuvred himself to the bed. 'She used tae be in your gran's circle at one time. Your gran couldnae stand her either. Nothing better tae do than mind other folks' business. She was aye poking her nose in.' He smiled. 'Big enough nose too. Face like the back end of a mongoose.'

He stood and placed both hands on the bed, shuffling until he was steady. Then slowly he eased himself onto the mattress and for some time after he sat without speaking, breathing harshly. His face was pale. When he looked around for his glass I passed it across to him. 'Soon be dinner time, Grandad.'

'Aye, son,' he said. 'Aye. Can you see my watch there?'

'Here.'

'It needs winding, son.'

The watch was weighty and gold and inscribed on the back with the name of the steelworks. It was a long service award and somewhere in my grandmother's sideboard there was a newspaper clipping of the presentation, fifty elderly gentlemen in suits and ties, looking up to a camera. Grandad was in the front row, bow-legged with his hands at his sides. The watch was thirty years old.

He said, 'I cannae wind it, son. I set it earlier on, but there's nae strength in my fingers.' He put down his glass and showed me a trembling hand. 'Weak as water.'

'It's just a bit fiddly,' I said.

'Aye.' He put a cigarette in his mouth. 'Aye, son.'

The match did not go out when he shook it but continued to burn in the ashtray. As he inhaled, the smoke caught in his throat and he started to cough. He reached behind his curtain for a glass beaker and brought up a mouthful of phlegm. For several minutes afterwards he continued to spit into the beaker. I concentrated on his watch, not wanting to look. When finally he stopped he said, 'I should fling these bloody things in the midden, Danny. It's a disease.' He held the cigarette between his forefinger and thumb, put it down on the edge of the ashtray. As he hid the beaker he said, 'Did I ever tell ye how it started, son?'

I shook my head. He had told me many times, and I had told the story at school, but I enjoyed the sound of his voice, the way his face and hands moved. A vet had prescribed them. He was playing football.

'I was keeping goal,' he said. 'We used to have a wee game in our lunch break there, depending on the weather, or maybe if orders were a bit slack. And I picked up a lot of cuts and bruises on my knees, here, from diving about in the gravel. Because it was a gravel yard we used to play on, near where the rolling mills used to be. This was before I came down to England, I was a young man then. And I took a run of boils on top of these cuts.'

He began to roll up his trouser leg, showing the knee, white and swollen. 'You can see the scars yet,' he said. 'So I went along tae the chemist, name of O'Brien. He was more of a vet than a chemist, a horse-doctor, ye know. And he says, *D'ye smoke, son?* I says, *No.* He says, *Did ye ever?* And, *No,* I says. Well these boils were festering, and they were spreading out, down the shin here, elbows too. And he diagnoses nerves. He says, *It's your nerves, wee man. It's a nervous complaint ye have.* So he sells me a tuppenny powder and he sends me next door. There was a tobacconist's there – a wee hole in the wall – and then a pork butcher next to that – he sold crackling at a ha'penny a bag. Well I bought a packet of Woodbines from this tobacconist, they were supposed to calm the nerves. I used to buy them in packs of five, or singles if I was hard up, and then it was tens and twenties and that was me, hooked for life. And it was a life sentence, so it was. I'd have been better off with a bag of crackling from the start!'

He rolled down his trouser leg and picked up his cigarette. A length of ash fell to his lap and he swiped it away, smearing his trousers.

'The boils didn't clear up for a long time anyway, and I'll tell ye something else, son. That was O'Brien's brother-in-law who sold me the baccy. The pair of bloody toerags, they were in cahoots all along, chemist and tobacconist! Well, I've no trusted a vet or a chemist since, and I'm no too keen on tobacconists either. Nerves, by Christ. It's nae bloody wonder!'

He laughed, and I said, 'Did you ever have to fetch a vet for the pigs, Grandad?'

'The pigs? Oh aye, many a time.' He leaned forwards to take his glass from the cabinet and picked up his cigarette. Grey hairs showed above the neck of his vest. He sipped loudly and said, 'Oh aye, ye have tae keep on good terms with the vet if you're going tae keep pigs. Or any beast come to that.'

I said, 'What about when you want to breed them?'

'Breed pigs?' He laughed wheezily. 'That's no a vet ye need, son!' His eyes held mine and when I smiled he said, 'Funny thing about the sows, Danny – they used to come on heat every three weeks, and from the day the boar served them till the day the litter arrived, that was three months, three weeks and three days exactly. All the threes!' I calculated in my mind that that would take us to mid-November. Grandad said, 'Have ye ever seen a boar's tackle, Danny? The prick's shaped like a corkscrew. So it is! Your gran used to feel awfy sorry for the poor sows. She was very soft-hearted in some ways.'

Grandad's eyes glazed and for a moment he faltered. When he stubbed out his cigarette I said, 'What about if I wanted to breed this pig?'

'This pig?' His face darkened. 'I think she's past it by now, Danny. No, I doubt you'd get any joy there.' He shook his head. 'No.' I wanted to press him, but waited. He said, 'Your gran wouldn't have liked the idea, son. I was all for selling the brute a long time ago, but she wouldnae have it. They were very attached, d'ye see? She wanted tae let it bide in peace. Because it was a good age even then, a real old-timer.' He winked. 'Like me and that watch – old-timers but good-timers. That's right, isn't it son?'

I nodded. His watch was beginning to stiffen. I pulled out the winder and reset the time by his alarm clock. As I gave it back to him I said, 'I've been going out to the cottage with a friend from school.'

'A school chum, aye?'

'We've been taking good care of her. And looking after the garden.'

'Aye.' His lips were wet from the whisky. He dabbed at his mouth with his handkerchief and glanced at the time.

'But we were thinking,' I said. 'We'll need to get some more straw and stuff, from the farmer.'

'The farmer,' he said vaguely.

'Ted,' I said. 'We don't know where to find him.'

Grandad eased the watch over his wrist. 'Ted? I think he

used to stay out by the old village, Danny. Somewhere over that way. Because he lost a lot of his land to the quarries ye know, the new quarries. That was a long time ago.' I waited whilst he lit another cigarette. He shook his head. 'But you see, they never found the same grade of ore, son, and that was part of the trouble. The percentages were all wrong. Too much clay.'

'You don't know if he's still there then?'

'Who's that?'

'Ted.'

'No, son,' he said. 'No. I couldn't tell ye, son.'

I nodded. In the long silence that followed I listened to the steady tick of his alarm clock. Grandad's face became blank, unseeing. His cigarette crackled as it burned. The smoke wound past his face in the sunlight. Finally I said, 'It'll soon be time for your dinner, Grandad.'

He squinted at the clock, then looked at his watch. 'Aye, son,' he said. He slipped a finger under the strap and rubbed at his wrist. 'It's yours ye know, Danny. The watch. I'll make sure it's put aside for ye.'

I nodded.

'Solid gold, ye know.'

He gazed at me until I said, 'Yes.'

TWENTY

WHEN THE clouds passed across us we hunched our shoulders, expecting rain, but none fell. The wind came in squalls and then there was sunshine, a sudden warmth. Surinder unzipped her jacket and I watched it flap open on the next gust of air. Her hair blew loose round her face and she combed it back with her fingers. I turned up my collar. It wasn't the best day to come but we had planned for it, made sandwiches. We ate them before we reached the first farm, sitting on a hillside beneath a clear sky. Our bicycles lay in a ditch by the side of the road. It turned cold before we opened our Coke cans.

In the farmyard we were surrounded by squabbling chickens, enclosed in a square of grey buildings. A dog came barking towards us from the shade of a doorway, dragging its chain over concrete. Surinder gripped my arm and I stood frozen until a woman appeared from the far side of a tractor. She was red-faced and smiling and wore a grey woollen cardigan, wellington boots, a flowered headscarf. There was a metal bucket looped over her arm. She scolded the dog and said, 'Sorry dears,' in an accent very different from ours. But she had never heard of a Ted. She led us back to the gate, ignoring the chickens, and recited the names of the other farms in her area. Then she pointed to a crossroads, a mini-roundabout, and said to follow the road to the right. 'There's a few up there I don't know much of.' As we pedalled away we waved to her and Surinder called, 'Thank you,' almost losing her steering.

No cars passed us in either direction but from the distance came a constant whisper of afternoon traffic. Behind the hedges, beyond ditches on both sides, there were fields of yellow and green, crops bending in the breeze. We cycled together and when Surinder braked to explore for flowers in a verge I stopped and waited, leaning my arms on the handlebars. Afterwards the road began to rise steeply and Surinder dismounted to push. She shouted into the wind, 'My legs are killing me!' and after a few minutes I doubled back to her side. As I got off my bike she said, 'Do you know, when they were recruiting for the Boer War three-quarters of the men got turned away because of flat feet?'

'That's interesting,' I said.

She nodded and held one hand to her chest, catching her breath. 'And bad teeth. That was in Manchester. Only it was two-thirds, not three-quarters. But,' she lifted a finger, smiling, 'when this medical officer in Bradford went to inspect the kids in this school he discovered not one of them had taken their clothes off in six months! Six months!'

I shrugged. 'So what's wrong with that?'

'It's disgusting. The English are so filthy!'

The pedals of our bicycles collided, and I said, 'So where'd you find all this out?'

'In the library, yesterday.'

'What's the point?'

'It's history! You're supposed to know your history!' She reached to her basket and shook the bundle of flowers in my face. A little while later she said, 'It's for next term, Danny. We're doing the Victorians, all of us, you included.'

'But we're not all swots,' I said. I gripped my brakes and climbed onto the bike, standing up in the saddle as I started to pedal.

'It beats hanging about the house all day,' she shouted.

'What's wrong with that?' I used my front wheel to balance, steadying myself on the pedals until Surinder came level. 'That's not so bad.'

'With Mum? And big brother from Birmingham, and big brother's little wifie?'

'No problem,' I said.

'What do you know! You've never met them, all they can talk about is weddings and babies.'

'Weddings and babies are interesting.'

She turned her wheel into mine and I began to tip sideways. 'Not to me they're not,' she said. 'Especially when the babies aren't even born yet. I'd rather read about scabby children in Bradford.'

'Swot,' I said.

Surinder smiled. She pointed into the breeze. 'There's a man with welly boots,' she said.

Where the hill began to level out in the distance there was a curve in the road and a Land-Rover parked at the gate to a field. The driver's door was open and the man sat with one foot placed outside on the ground. He was writing in a notebook. I said to Surinder, 'It's your turn to ask,' but she shook her head and lingered behind me. I approached him alone, pushing the bike at my side. Because I did not know what to say I stood where he would see me and waited. The man stared out to the field, rapidly counting. He wore a cravat beneath his anorak, green wellingtons, brown corduroys. On the seat beside him there was a chequered cap and a newspaper, a pair of binoculars. 'Yes?' he said finally. He made a tick on his page.

'I was wondering,' I said. I scratched my nose. 'We're looking for a farmer called Ted. We were wondering if maybe you knew him, where he lives or anything. If you could point us in the right direction?'

'A farmer called Ted?' He screwed the cap on his pen and glanced at Surinder. 'Does Ted have a surname?' he asked me.

'I don't know.' I looked over my shoulder and Surinder started to grin. She turned away from me. 'I mean, I don't know what it is. But he's quite old now.'

The man nodded. He tapped his pen on the dashboard. When he spoke he sounded as if he was repeating himself, as if others were listening. 'Well, I don't know if I can be of much use to you. Most of the land around here is my own, or my family's, and to the best of my knowledge there are no Teds, young or old, in the immediate vicinity. Certainly not farmers. I dare say you might stumble on someone of that name, but not anyone I would know.'

I said, 'Have you lived around here very long?'

He raised an eyebrow, closed his notebook with one hand. I could smell his aftershave, petrol fumes from his car. 'A considerable period,' he said.

'And you own all this?' I looked across at his fields, the distant hedges, dead elm trees. A bank of grey cloud was thickening on the horizon.

'As far as the church spire,' he said. 'Somewhat further

behind us.' He lifted his foot inside the car and reached for the door handle. He was waiting, faintly smiling.

I nodded. 'Well thanks anyway,' I said.

He turned the key in his ignition. 'No trouble at all,' he said, and pulled the door shut.

'Too fucking right,' said Surinder.

From the crest of the hill it was possible to pick out the white dot of my grandparents' cottage, earth-piles and factories, the old site of the steelworks. Below us there stretched a thick mat of woodland, and beyond that the start of the quarries. I saw a bird hovering over a field, a grain silo in the distance, several long prefabricated buildings. Surinder pointed and said, 'There's the next farm,' and we began to descend, the wind beating against us. She let go of her handful of flowers and we turned to see them scattering on the tarmac. We met another slight incline and started to pedal. 'So do you want to know about Glasgow?' Surinder asked.

'What about it?'

'This is the 1880s.' She took a deep breath. 'And you had so many people in so few houses, you'd get three or four families all living in the same room. They had to sleep in the cupboards, or under the beds, anywhere. So the Council came along and stuck tickets outside the doors, saying how many could live there, and then they paid these people to go around in the middle of the night hammering on the doors, just to make sure they were all legal. They wouldn't have anywhere to hide. Can you imagine it?'

'That's where my grandad came from,' I said.

'That's why I'm telling you. He might remember it.'

'He's not that ancient.'

'Near enough.' We passed an electricity sub-station, and a sign saying *LeisureLand*, half-obscured by branches and leaves. Like the other hoardings it had been erected in the spring, two years before, and now the paint was beginning to peel, the colours were fading. Surinder continued, 'They all lived in flats anyway, proper flats made out of stone and everything – tenements – not like your estate, but they had to share a single toilet out on the landing. All these people using the same toilets, they got blocked up and overflowed down the stairs. Disgusting. And you'd get the kids running about with no shoes on, so they caught dysentery and all sorts. Talk about India!' A few yards further on the road curved sharply away and there was another board, nailed to a tree, which said *No Trespassers*. We slowed to a stop and looked back in the direction we had come, the shaded bend in the road. I saw the white paint of the grain silo flickering through the trees. 'This way,' I said. A side road met ours beyond the next turning, its entrance crossed by a cattle-grid. Yellow and black painted stones followed the line of the kerb. 'Shall we go up?'

'I suppose so,' Surinder said.

'It's your turn to ask, remember.'

'Not if I don't want to.'

A channel of grass ran down the centre of the road. We cycled on either side of it, our heads bowed, not talking. The tarmac was rutted and broken and both verges fell steeply to ditches. The air smelled of dampness, pigs somewhere in the distance. Before we could reach any buildings a man in blue overalls came out to meet us. He was wiping his hands on a rag. He called something inaudible, then shouted again, shaking his head. 'We've got none,' he said. 'You're wasting your time.'

'Sorry?'

He stopped in the centre of the road, tucked the rag in his top pocket. 'Work. We've none.'

'No,' I said. I climbed from my bike. 'We're looking for

someone. A farmer called Ted. We were wondering if you knew him.'

'Who?'

'Ted,' said Surinder.

'Ted who?'

'We're not sure,' I said, 'he was a friend of my gran's.'

'Was he?' For several seconds the man stared at Surinder, then said to me, 'And doesn't your gran know where he lives?'

'No,' I said. 'She's dead.'

The man nodded but his face didn't change. He looked at me calmly, and finally said, 'Well, let's put it like this, son, you won't find him by trespassing on private property, that's for certain. And you won't find him if you don't know his fucking name. But you can take it from me, there's no Ted working here, and there's definitely no jobs going. I'd be the first to know, either way.'

He drew a deep breath and after a moment I realized we were expected to leave. I shrugged my shoulders. As I turned the handlebars of my bicycle I said, 'I don't suppose there's any chance you'd sell us some straw?'

'Straw?'

'We've got this pig,' I said.

'Who has?'

'Us two.'

The man laughed. He shook his head. From behind us I heard a car shifting down through its gears, rattling over the cattle grid. Surinder said, 'It's that guy in his jeep again,' and she moved her bike to the side of the road. The Land-Rover flashed its headlamps. The man in the overalls raised his hand in salute.

'Well, if you have got a pig,' he said, still watching the car, 'I'll tell you now you won't get rid of it. No one will touch it. What do you feed it?'

'Swill.'

'Do you have a certificate?'

'No.'

'You'd best get one. And if you're planning to move it make sure the veterinary know.'

'They do,' I said.

I had no idea what he meant. He looked at me and smiled. As the Land-Rover drew up beside us he tapped twice on its bonnet and turned to walk back to the silo. 'It's definitely not straw you're wanting, sunshine,' he said. 'That's the last thing you need.'

The man in the car was wearing his cap and speaking to me before I could hear him. He leant across to lower his window and I bent towards my reflection. I smiled politely. As the window came down there was a sound of violins, a woman's voice singing softly. The man switched off the tape. 'I said you are on private property and I'd be grateful if you would remove yourself and your companion immediately. I'm sure you have homes to go to.'

'We're just leaving,' I said. Surinder was cycling back to the main road. She disappeared from view as the Land-Rover pulled smoothly away in the other direction. The man's gaze was fixed directly ahead. His rear lights were shining red. For some time after the car had departed I remained standing on the side of the road, staring at nothing. Then the rain came. The ruts in the road filled quickly with water. As I pushed off to follow Surinder I found my front tyre was punctured.

TWENTY-ONE

SURINDER WAITED for me at the *LeisureLand* hoarding. She was hugging herself beneath the shelter of a beech tree. Rain bounced from the road. My punctured tyre flapped on the tarmac. I quickened my pace, pulling the bike at my side, and as I drew closer I called, 'Where did you get to?'

Her shrug was dismissive. She held her palm to the sky. 'How are we supposed to get back?'

'You should've heard him,' I said.

'Danny, I don't care.' She rounded her shoulders and shivered. Her anorak was almost transparent, glistening wet. 'I want to go home now,' she said.

'But what about Ted?'

'Ted who?' She held my gaze. 'It's a dead loss, Danny.'

I looked away. Droplets of rain fell from the leaves. A

smear of grey cloud descended from the crest of the hill. I
said, 'It'll probably pass in a minute or two, it's easing off
already.'

'It won't, Danny.' She stared until I was forced to look
at her. 'It's going to get worse, and you've got a flat
tyre.'

'So how do we get home?' I said.

'You tell me.'

'Same way as we got here?' I suggested.

'It's miles!' The rain turned heavy again. Surinder looked
over her shoulder, into the trees. 'We can go through here,'
she said.

'Riding the bikes?'

'Forget the bikes! We can hide them somewhere, come
back when the weather's better, tomorrow or something.
I'm not hanging around here to catch pneumonia, Danny,
and I'm not walking home in the rain.' She gathered her
hair in a twist and tucked it inside her jacket. As she pulled
her zip to her chin she said, 'Coming?'

I shrugged, not moving, but when she guided Gran's
bike beneath the *LeisureLand* hoarding I followed her. We
forced our way through a tangle of bushes and trees and
came to the remains of a wall, a tumble of stones, beyond
which the land dipped suddenly and the trees became
taller. We laid the bicycles on their sides beneath a clump of
tall ferns. I tried to break off some stalks to disguise them
but Surinder called me to hurry. The ground was damp
and spongy and as the undergrowth thinned we passed
through mouldering piles of litter and clothes, burnt tree
trunks, the remains of a den. I picked up a page from a
magazine, stuck with insects and seeds. Its sheen was dulled
and the colours were bleached almost to white, but I could
see clearly the shape of a woman. She was black, lying
naked on a bed. There were other pages strewn ahead of us,

most of them ripped, parts of pictures. Surinder waited for me. 'What is it?' she asked.

I held out the sheet and she took it. At first it wasn't obvious. She turned the page at an angle, and looked at the back, then recognition showed in her eyes and she let it fall to the ground. She wiped her fingers on my jacket. 'Where's all the nice badgers and squirrels and things?'

I said, 'Richard starts his job here next week.'

'In the woods?'

'*LeisureLand.*'

We clambered up a bank, clutching at 'tree roots. 'It doesn't exist,' she said. She was breathless and we paused for a moment.

'They're starting on Monday,' I said.

She imitated my brother, talking as if through a cold. 'Yeah, labouring or somefink, it's alright but it's peanuts, Danny, yeah.' She walked in front of me. 'Only you told me he was a cook, so how come he's not selling hotdogs or burgers or something?'

'Who to?'

'The other labourers.'

'They don't exist,' I said.

We waded through a stretch of tall grass and nettles, our hands raised in the air, and finally emerged to a clearing, the edge of a lake. It was stinking and black, huge swirls of oil on its surface, glistening like metal. A dead tree stood at its centre, stark against the grey sky. The rain had become a drizzle. I kicked a stone at the water and Surinder asked me, 'Which way's home then?'

'It's your shortcut.'

She gestured towards a ridge of red soil in the distance. 'Over there maybe?'

'Maybe.'

I allowed her to take my hand and we walked away from

the water, along a pathway of rubble that skirted several other smaller lakes. We passed signs which said *Slurry Only* and as my eyes travelled back along the loops and lines of the oil I realized the stench was the smell my father used to bring home. We were close to the quarries. I patted my pockets for cigarettes, drew one from its box and held it in my palm.

At the ridge we found a pathway. I went first and Surinder said, 'So what does your brother do exactly, when he's not puking up?'

'Nothing. He sits on his bum. Mum battered him for not coming to the funeral on time, so now he does the hoovering to make up to her, but the rest of the time he just lies about.'

'Like you then?'

'I do plenty,' I said. 'I'm a man of the soil.'

'But when are you going to read the textbooks, Danny, and start making notes, and all that kind of stuff?'

'The books are under my bed,' I told her.

'And?'

'Looking after the pig is real work.'

'And?'

'Eventually,' I said. 'Maybe.'

'You'll end up like him,' she said.

The wind at the top of the ridge gusted fiercely against us and I didn't reply. Surinder's jacket flattened over her chest, flapped loudly on her sleeves. I stood behind her and leant my chin on her shoulder. She stepped back into my arms, pressing against me. We faced a landscape heaped with scrap metal and rubble. Everywhere there were piles of cemented bricks, rusting pipes and swarf coils. Corrugated iron sheets sliced through mounds of red earth. A crane had been abandoned close by and from its hook hung an engine, suspended a few feet from the ground. I saw a tin hat lying upended, cupping green water, and a stiff rubber glove, like a hand in the soil.

In the damp wind I couldn't light my cigarette and I went to crouch in the lee of the crane. We began walking, our heads down, and I said, 'What about your brother, when's he going back?'

'A couple of days, a couple of weeks. Don't know. He never says.'

'He's the doctor?'

'No! He's the same as Dad, another bloody grocer.' I held out the cigarette and she shook her head. 'The doctor's the one that lives in America, the hippy. I've told you. He used to lock himself in the toilet and smoke cannabis. Then he stopped wearing his turban and went back to India in search of natural remedies. He hates pills, he won't prescribe them. Whenever we see him he's always shouting at Mum about it. She takes pills for everything.'

'So does mine,' I said. 'I used to think that's where babies came from, you took a pill to have a baby.'

'You'd get on with Raminder then. He's full of stupid ideas.'

'Who's Raminder?'

'The doctor!'

We passed an old sink, a pair of boots without laces. In the distance before us I could see the remains of a farm building. It stood alone at the head of a rise, stone built and roofless. The sky was visible through two windows. I said, 'So why is the other brother staying at your house?'

'He's taking a holiday or something. He wants to show off his wife before she gets all fat and pregnant.' She shrugged, and took the cigarette from my fingers. 'I don't know. Someone tried to burn down his shop last week. They poured petrol in the letter box.'

I looked at her face as we walked, but she didn't say any more. Finally I said, 'Why didn't you tell me?' and touched her arm, trying to stop her. She continued to walk, not glancing back. 'Surinder!' I called.

'What!' She half turned, lifted her hands in the air. 'I just didn't,' she said.

I hurried after her, matching my pace to hers. She handed me the last of the cigarette and turned her face to the distance, looking at nothing. Quietly I said, 'Was anyone hurt?'

'No. Everyone's fine.'

'Do the police know?'

'Probably.'

'Probably?'

'Yes.' She patted my arm and said, 'I told you, all they ever talk about is weddings and babies. I don't know anything about it.'

I shook my head, flicked the cigarette at the breeze. It flared for a moment, landed dead in the soil. Surinder looked to the ground and placed her feet carefully between the puddles. As we approached the farm building I said, 'Why won't you talk about it?'

She entered the building without responding. Inside seemed no darker than out. Wood lintels and frames enclosed empty doorways, the windows were smashed. A few joists crossed where the roof would have been and parts of the walls had begun to collapse. A black scorch mark in one corner suggested a fireplace, but there were no other traces of occupation, no electrical fittings or plumbing, no wallpaper. There was a scattering of straw on the ground. I picked up a stalk and drew it along the side of her face. 'Surinder?'

'Danny!' She turned suddenly, snatching the straw from my hand. Her eyes were wet and when she spoke her voice was unsteady. 'There is nothing to tell. No one got hurt. No one knows who did it. The police don't give a fuck anyway, and there's no point in going on about it. So just let it drop.'

'Who's going on about it? I only asked . . .' But Surinder wasn't listening. She walked away and stood in the rear doorway, leaning into the frame, her arms folded. The stiffness of her pose told me she was angry, and as I watched her I also became angry, until finally I said, 'Fuck you then!' and turned in the other direction.

Outside I stood with my back to the wall. The sky above was grey as far as the horizon, the clouds barely moving. I blew on my hands and tucked them under my arms. After some minutes I went to a corner of the building and pulled myself onto a window ledge. I climbed to the level of the lowest wall, nine or ten feet from the ground, and eased myself upright. The wind whipped against me as slowly I picked a way round to the far side of the building. Surinder glanced up but she didn't acknowledge me. When I was standing directly above her I crouched and sat down. We were facing out to the first of the quarries. The rocks appeared blue, and then grey, gouged in layers to a bed of red sludge and crisscrossed with tyre tracks. Shadows crept over the contours. I saw a glint of water, a plastic bag caught in the wind. Nothing else moved.

'Do you suppose this is Ted's house?' I said finally. Surinder didn't reply. Holding tightly to the wall I leaned forwards until I could see her. 'Are you not talking to me now?'

After a long pause she said, 'No,' and continued to stare at the quarry.

I sat upright. 'I'm sorry,' I said.

'Good.'

'Do you want to talk about bad housing in Glasgow?'

'Fuck off.'

'Weddings and babies?'

'It's no joke, Danny.' She turned inside the wall and sat down, drew her knees to her chin. She looked up at the roof beams. 'Dad is convinced I won't last till I'm eighteen,' she said. 'He thinks it's a natural instinct and every girl's just dying to get married so she can start making babies.'

'You don't have to be married for that.'

'Or else all we're really interested in is lipstick and make-up and buying little things to put in the house. We're desperate for a husband so we can start painting our faces.'

'Sounds more like it.'

'Who wants to paint their face? Or spend all day dusting the furniture? Honestly, a career's the only way out, become a teacher or something. A doctor, like Raminder.'

'Would they let you become a doctor?'

'Why not?' she sighed. 'Our daughter the intellectual, they'd love it. They just won't admit it.'

'You're not doing the right subjects,' I said. I eased my legs over the wall, preparing to drop between two roof beams. 'You'd have to take sciences.'

'A teacher then.'

'What of?'

'History!'

As I pushed myself clear I glimpsed my grandparents' cottage, the white sheds of the Enterprise Zone. I landed heavily and the cigarettes jerked from my jacket pocket. A splash of rain hit the ground beside them. 'History teachers are wankers though.'

'I wouldn't be.' She waited until I had lit a cigarette, and said, 'Do one for me.'

We sat on either side of the doorway, our feet drawn back from the rain. The sky had darkened above us. I said, 'If they'd love it if you were a doctor and they'd love it if you were married, why don't you do both?'

'Why should I?' She leant her head on the wall, then said, 'Mum reckons it's companionship. They all do. She says it's the only way to be happy, settle down and be part of some family. It's not like she's over the moon herself. All she ever does is shout and argue and chuck things around the house. It drives you crazy. One day they'll just explode or something.'

'Not all families are like that.'

'Yours I suppose?'

'At least Richard's not a hippy.'

'He's just a fascist.' The rain fell in large blotches, spattering the far wall. I held my cigarette at arm's length and watched as the paper dampened, began to disintegrate. When I let it fall from my hand Surinder passed me hers. She said, 'Mum's so sure I'm going to get married she's got this fortune stashed away in India. All rupees. Just sitting in a bank account. She's determined I'm going to marry this guy from her village in India. We've even got his photo pinned up in the kitchen.'

'You've never mentioned it.'

'He's a fat creep.'

I looked at Surinder across the open doorway. She stared into space, her eyelids heavy, her chin resting on her knees. I tried to imagine her differently, as the wife of someone I didn't know, and I said, 'But you're not going to get married, are you?'

'Not to you anyway.'

'I didn't mean me.'

She looked round, gazed at me steadily. 'Why not?'

I said, 'I thought we were talking about this guy pinned in your kitchen.'

'In other words, you don't want to.'

'What?'

'Marry me.'

I stood up. 'We're going to get soaked,' I said. 'Shall we go back?'

'We'll get even wetter!'

'We can dry out in the cottage. It's not far now. Come on.'

'Not until you answer.'

'Surinder!'

She wrapped her arms round her legs. 'You wanted to talk about marriage and babies.'

I stared down at her. I was shivering. A minute passed, or more, and I said, 'Are you coming or not?' She didn't reply and I began to walk without her, quickly at first, but the soil became waterlogged and began to pull at my heels. When I tried to hurry I slipped and fell forwards, landed with my palms on either side of a puddle. As I stood I looked back and saw her small in the distance, picking a way through the mud, her arms folded over her chest. I shouted for her to hurry but she didn't look up. I turned and walked on, hunching my shoulders in the rain.

TWENTY-TWO

O NE AFTERNOON in the following week I returned to the woods for the bicycles. Surinder did not want to come with me. She said she was going to spend a day in the library, reading about the Victorians, the British Empire. She said I ought to go with her, she would meet me at the bus stop. I nodded and said 'Maybe,' but instead I went to the cottage. I ate my lunch in the kitchen with a school book on the table beside me. Crumbs fell on the pages but I didn't read what was beneath them. I wasn't interested. As I drank my tea I watched a cloud of small flies circling above the lid of the swill pot. Brown beetles fed on the splashes at the foot of the cooker and a mould had begun to form against one skirting board. Before I left for the quarries I wiped a damp cloth over the table, emptied my crumbs in the sink.

The soil was dry now, the air still and warm. I walked quickly, looking directly ahead, and when I came to the first of the earth ridges I forced my way to the top without pausing. I hadn't thought how I would manage to return home with both bicycles, only of showing them to Surinder, cleaned and repaired. Looking out from the ridge I realized I could not bring them across this land. In the distance there were groups of workmen, lorries and mechanical diggers. I supposed they were going to begin clearing the debris, flattening the earth-piles. It was too far to recognize Richard. I slid down the next slope, the rubble falling after me, and broke into a run. The stench of the lakes came suddenly. I saw a dead animal, its fur matted with oil, and held a hand over my face. When I found the place where we'd emerged from the nettles I was dizzy and sweating. I paused and crouched down, catching my breath. I lit a cigarette when my head cleared.

Under the cover of the branches there was dampness. The light fell in patches, glowing from the algae on the bark of the trees. I noticed clusters of flowers, bright red fungi, a pile of old bedclothes. There were crisp packets and beer cans. Several times I thought I recognized a particular tree or dip in the land, a route through the saplings and undergrowth, but each time I found myself wading deeper into the woods. Then I found a ball of crumpled paper, a page from a magazine, the picture I had shown to Surinder. Through a gap in the bushes ahead I could see the remains of the den we had passed, and as I headed towards it I noticed a length of corrugated plastic large enough to have been its roof, a broken deckchair and some kitchen utensils. The trench in the ground was several feet deep and its floor was covered with carpet. A stack of wet newspapers sat in a corner. I stood at the edge and jumped down.

Not long after we had moved to our estate some older

boys had taken me to a similar den. I was supposed to be their prisoner. The den was hidden in some woods beyond the school playing fields, on a piece of land that would soon become houses. The only source of light was the entrance, a hole in the ground which they had concealed with branches. There was a length of broken ladder inside and strips of wallpaper had been pegged to one wall. A line of stones on the floor prevented the paper curling upwards. It was cold and damp and smelling of clay, and when I started to cry the boys told me to guard the entrance instead. They sat below in the gloom as if waiting for something, reading from a pile of comics. Afterwards I was sworn to secrecy and warned that I mustn't return alone. But I didn't go back. The following weekend I tried to dig my own bunker in my grandmother's garden. Grandad told me if I went deep enough I might come out in Australia. My grandmother said that India was nearer.

The newspapers piled in this den were sodden and when I kicked away the top copies I saw they were identical. It was an old edition of the local free paper. The front page had a drawing of the *LeisureLand* site, another article about the jobs that were coming. I bent closer. It was on the front page because the owners had changed. They were no longer Dutch, but local; a consortium of local businessmen. They were going to build a life-sized iron foundry with authentic noises and smells, perhaps also an underground coal mine. The surrounding land would be developed for housing, new supermarkets and factories, a water-sports complex. An application had been made for a rail-link. The carpet squelched beneath me. It was mouldy. I stood on the newspapers and with an effort I managed to climb out.

Beyond the next rise the bicycles were clearly visible in the ferns. I picked away the leaves that were trapped in the wheel-spokes, pushed the bikes separately through the trees to the road. With a bike on each side of me I gripped the handlebars and set off in the direction I had come with Surinder. But before I reached the electricity sub-station a car came round the corner towards me, blaring its horn as it swerved outwards. I crossed to the other side of the road. Another car was approaching, and behind it a Land-Rover. I recognized the farmer. His window was open, bare elbow protruding. I heard the music on his hi-fi and watched as he passed me. He didn't look round.

On the flat roads it was possible to pedal my grandmother's bicycle and guide Grandad's with my right hand, but the punctured tyre made progress slow and the bikes often skewed apart, colliding when I tried to steady them. There was no easy way to grip both handlebars and I struggled to control the steering when I began to descend. I had to dismount as the ground became steeper, and paused frequently to straighten my back, several times swapping the bicycles round. In the dry air of the road my throat became sore and my mouth tasted sourly of cigarettes, but I hadn't thought to bring money and when I asked at a garage for water the attendant shook his head and ignored me. There were bruises on my shins from the pedals. Blisters were beginning to form on my feet. Fifty yards from the garage I threw down the bikes in frustration and sat on the bank at the side of the road.

As the cars and trucks sped past me I thought about Surinder, the photograph in her kitchen. I tried to picture a wedding in India, traditional dress, jewellery, her father's shop closed in the precinct. I imagined walking towards her as she came through the estate. She was pushing a pram, wearing make-up, a sari. Her hands and face were darker, tanned from a summer in India, as they had been the previous summer. She glanced at me quickly and looked down. I whispered her name but she shook her head and hurried away from me. After a moment I followed at a distance and waited on the wall outside her house. It was pouring with rain. I hunched my shoulders and remained where I was sitting, not expecting her to appear, satisfied that she could see me. But when I tried to imagine a conversation between us we were both smiling. She described her marriage, called her husband a creep, and laughed when I told her about the new pigs I had bought. I explained about the boar, the smell it gives off, the shape of its tackle.

For a minute or more the road was clear. I picked up the bicycles and started to walk. The air in Gran's garden would be noisy with pigs. I saw several long sheds, a big wheel and a fun fair in the distance. I pictured Surinder as she drew up to the gate in a car. She unfastened her seatbelt and reached behind for a briefcase, grinned and waved when she saw me. She was wearing a skirt, a hairband, heels that clicked on the kitchen linoleum when she followed me indoors. I wiped my hands on a rag and filled the kettle to make tea. She hung her scarf on the back of the door and pulled off her shoes. She began to massage her foot, describing her day as I lit a cigarette for each of us. But then I couldn't think what we would say. I tried to recall our conversation in the house by the quarries, but the effort was too great. As the afternoon lengthened I found I could think about nothing at all. Once I passed a field of stubble and straw bales. I concentrated on the road a few feet ahead of the bicycles, made no attempt to remember its location. Perhaps I knew then that I wouldn't return. My legs were heavy and several times I stumbled. The objects around me shimmered, too bright to look at. When finally I arrived at the cottage I dropped the bikes on the front lawn and lay face down beside them.

The sweat on my forehead was cold when I woke. My

arms were bent beneath me and my shoulders were aching. I rose and walked into the house, drank from the tap in the bathroom. I stood and gazed at myself in the mirror. The texture of the grass was etched on the side of my face. In the previous weeks my complexion had deepened, become redder, and there were freckles on the bridge of my nose. My hair was thicker and lighter now. I leaned closer, examining the lines round my eyes. If I clenched my teeth and frowned I looked older. I opened the buttons on my shirt and took a step backwards, inhaling as I pushed my hands in my pockets. My shoulders were narrow, the skin smooth and pale on my chest. I stepped out of my shoes and ran the tap at the sink until the water felt tepid. I took off my clothes and washed myself down with a flannel.

It was almost teatime when I left the cottage for home. I fed the pig early, the last of the slops from the pot and three cups of pellets from a sack in the conservatory. I wedged the plastic swill tub in the basket of Gran's bicycle. It was becoming mouldy, needing washing, and as I pedalled into the breeze I caught a faint smell of vegetables. The air was cooler now and rippled in the arms of my shirt. Sunlight glinted from the approaching windshields. Many of the cars trailed boats and caravans, carried racing cycles on the roof-racks. I passed a family eating sandwiches at a table on the side of the road, a group of small boys carrying jam jars and nets. The smallest boy was pissing into a milk bottle. His trousers were round his ankles. As I turned off the dual carriageway I glanced behind me, saw the boy hurrying after his friends, holding the bottle aloft. They paused for a moment and then scattered.

In the older estates of the town there were wide open spaces, swing parks and playing fields. I saw children in swimsuits, old people sitting in deckchairs. A man in a vest and shorts nodded from his front garden as I passed him. I took a short cut through a narrow alley-way, heard lawn-mowers on either side of me, a radio playing from an upstairs window. Looking over a fence I glimpsed a pair of tanned legs on a sunbed, a rabbit sitting in the grass. Then I turned into Surinder's street and saw Spider and Stan ahead of me, waiting on the wall opposite her house.

TWENTY-THREE

A T SCHOOL it was only the teachers who had called them by their real names. They were supposed to be cousins, although they looked very different. Most of the stories about them concerned fights and arguments, damage to buildings, police being called to the school. I knew that they lived on the far edge of the estate, in a long row of prefabricated houses which backed onto the playing fields. From time to time I had seen them running across the fields during lessons, jumping the fence in the distance, disappearing into the gardens. I always saw them together and they had few other friends. Most people tried to avoid them.

As I came towards Surinder's house on the bicycle I tried to pedal faster, hoping to pass them, but the bike was too heavy and old, it barely accelerated. The chain-guard rattled when I hit a hole in the road and both boys looked round. Spider got to his feet and pushed his hands in his pockets, yawned as he stepped down from the kerb. I tried to steer round him but he moved sharply to stop me. He held onto the handlebars and smiled, and I saw that his teeth were stained yellow, chipped almost to points. The wheel shook when he poked it. 'Where'd you find this heap?' he said.

'It was my gran's,' I told him.

'Looks it,' he said, and I watched as he prised away the lid of the swill tub. He bent it back on itself, forced it into the side of basket. 'Meals on wheels?' he asked me. I shook my head and he turned towards Stan. 'Meals on wheels, Stan!' he said.

'Curry,' said Stan, and sat with his shoulders hunched forwards, resting his arms on his knees. The sun slanted low across the chimneys behind him and cast long blocks of shadow to each side of us. He jerked his chin at my pockets. 'Got any fags?' he said.

'I don't smoke.'

'Yes you do.' He shook his head and looked down. He was taller and thinner than Spider, with cropped blonde hair and a ring in one ear. Dark freckles marked his forehead and arms. Red insects teemed around his feet in the shade of the wall. He dropped a large gob of spittle beside them. 'We've seen you,' he said, and rubbed his boot in the spit. 'You and that girl you hang around with.'

I didn't reply, and Spider said, 'That's where she lives, you know. Over there.'

I shrugged, not looking. 'Does she?'

'We reckon she's your girlfriend, don't we Stan?'

'We're in the same classes at school,' I said.

'Classes,' Spider repeated. He pushed at the bell on my handlebars but the springs inside were rusty and the cogs jammed together. He began to unscrew the metal cap. 'What's that supposed to mean?'

'They're intellectuals,' Stan told him. 'They just talk about things.'

'You ought to go for it,' Spider said, and offered the cap on his upturned palm, keeping it just out of my reach. 'Paki women love it.' I tried to hold his gaze but his face hardened. He narrowed his eyes and spat from the side of his mouth.

'He's going red,' said Stan, and started to laugh.

I took a deep breath and faced away from them. At the entrance to our estate an old man was shuffling towards us. He was wearing his carpet slippers and carrying a shopping bag. As he came into the sunlight he made a salute and shook the bag in the air. It was full of bottles. He had been to my grandmother's funeral. As he turned into a garden I waved, and Spider looked over his shoulder. 'Meals on wheels!' he laughed, and tossed the cap at my chest. I caught it before it fell to the ground. 'There's some pakis moving into your square anyway,' he said. 'Next to where you live. We just saw them.'

'They're swarming all over the place,' said Stan. He got to his feet and stretched out his arms, took a packet of cigarettes from his back pocket. 'Your brother doesn't like them much, does he?'

'I wouldn't know.'

'Says they smell,' he said.

Spider watched as I screwed the cap on my bell. My hands were trembling. 'You should ask him,' he said, and showed his teeth, smiling. I started to pedal, expecting to be obstructed, but neither boy moved. As I passed the old man's house I heard a dog barking at the window, and the man shouting at it to be quiet.

★

A brick resounded from the wooden boards that protected the windows and spun across the pavement. Three boys chased it as if it were a football, trying to shoulder each other aside. In the passageway next to the bungalow two young women were talking, an empty pushchair between them. The boys ran past them and disappeared through the next square. I propped my bicycle beneath our front window. Richard was sitting on the doorstep in his T-shirt and shorts, a bottle of lemonade at his feet, cigarettes and matches beside it. He was wearing his shoes, but no socks, and the fronts of his legs were sunburnt. As I chained the back wheel of the bike I said, 'What's going on?'

He shrugged. 'Pakis moving next door,' he said. 'Other than that, not a lot.'

I waited. On the opposite side of the square an old woman was watching around her net curtains. I saw her most days coming back from the supermarket, carrying a tin of dog food, two bottles of beer. She always appeared to be frowning, worried about something. As I looked at her now she drew back into her room but didn't let go of the curtains. Her hand was bony, clenched tight.

Richard yawned, and said, 'Some guys from the Council came round this afternoon and took the padlock off. Dad says they were inside for hours, drilling and hammering. He's pissed off because he couldn't get his kip. Then these pakis turn up and the noise stops, just like that. They must've knocked off for the day.' He looked up. 'They've been backwards and forwards a couple of times anyway. Last time there was half a dozen of them, all jabbering away. Now there's just the two.'

In the farthest corner of the square a short, fat man stepped onto his porch. The windows beside him were leaded, like a house in the country, the curtains patterned with roses. He nodded to my brother and pushed his hands in his pockets. There was a chain round his neck and he wore a white tracksuit, blue trainers. The sunlight glinted from his spectacles.

'I'm telling you,' Richard said quietly, 'we should've got something together for this. It's pathetic. Everyone's watching, nothing's happening.'

'Like what?'

'Anything. Christ's sake.' He drank from his bottle, stared at the writing on the label. From inside our living room I could hear my mother coughing. I leant around Richard to see her. She was sitting in Dad's corner of the sofa, a coffee mug on the carpet beside her. Richard said, 'A couple of your mates were round earlier, Danny. Tapping me for matches. They reckoned they were going to burn down the bungalow.' He scratched at the sunburn on his legs. The skin was peeling.

'And what did you say to them?' I asked.

'I told them I didn't mind, but they ought to be careful. If they torch that place we'll fry as well.'

'Very funny,' I said.

Richard laughed, and called to the man in the tracksuit, 'New neighbours, Pete!'

'They'll be sizing the place up for conversions,' the man replied, and began walking towards us. His feet were splayed and he kept his hands in his pockets. As he drew nearer he said, 'You wait, Rich, soon as the pakis move in they have to get the lavs changed.' My brother smiled, and the man said to me, 'Your mum indoors, Danny?'

'I'm here, Pete,' she said, and came to stand in the hallway behind us. She gathered her cardigan around her as if she were cold. 'Your dinner's in the fridge, Danny,' she said. 'Salad.'

I nodded, and Pete said, 'I see you're getting some new neighbours, Jean, some of our ethnic cousins. I was telling

Richard, they'll be getting a new loo put in. They have to have two – the Muslims won't use the same facilities.'

'They might not be Muslims,' I said.

'Same difference,' he told me, and said to Mum, 'I wouldn't like it next door to us, anyway, Jean. My sister had it both sides, and it was sewing-machines twenty-four hours a day.' He lowered his voice and stepped closer, pushed his spectacles to the bridge of his nose. 'She called out the police in the end, but they turned round and said if she didn't keep quiet they'd arrest her for breach of the peace. How about that? You can't say anything.'

My mother shook her head. Across the square the old woman looked quickly in both directions and stepped backwards. Her hand released its grip on the curtains. Mum said, 'Yes, well,' and turned to go back indoors. 'Are you eating or not, Danny?'

'In a minute,' I said. The two women with the pushchair separated and left in different directions, walking quickly, as if they had meant to leave sooner. Richard screwed the cap on his bottle and gathered his cigarettes and matches. He was about to stand when we heard voices from the bungalow. The door was set back in a recess and for some time no one appeared. There were several locks and we listened as each one was fastened, a bunch of keys jangling heavily. Finally a young woman stepped backwards onto the pavement. She wore a long red-patterned tunic, baggy trousers gathered in at the ankle. The man had a beard, a grey jerkin, jeans which were covered in dust. The woman took his arm and for a moment they hesitated, not sure which way to go, then the woman decided to come towards us. The man looked ahead at the pavement. He had a long slow stride and his legs were bowed. I waited until the woman looked up, her eyes quickly scanning our faces, and smiled, 'Hello.'

She smiled back. 'Hello.' The man glanced round and nodded.

We watched until they had left us, Pete standing with his hands on his hips, my brother still clutching his bottle. 'Muslims,' Pete said. 'Told you.'

Richard said, 'Fuck's sake, Danny. Hello?'

I went indoors. My mother was facing the television, but the volume was off. It was a quiz programme, the faces silently speaking and laughing. She said, 'They've gone then?'

'Yes.'

She nodded. A woman in a sparkling red dress changed the numbers on a scoreboard. 'Did you see your grandad today, Danny?'

'Dinnertime.'

'How was he? Alright?'

I shrugged. 'Same as usual.'

'I should try and see him more,' she said. 'He shouldn't be in there, not really.'

'I suppose not,' I said, and went through to the kitchen.

TWENTY-FOUR

AN INSECT buzzed close to my ear and I flapped out an arm, suddenly waking. It drifted away to the ceiling, skimming the surface, and came to rest near the window. After a while I realized there were many others. I reached to my side and took a paperback from Surinder's bag, a library book with a plastic cover. I rose to my feet. The ceiling was low and I was able to reach it almost without jumping, but the angle was awkward and the insects scattered away to the walls. I stalked them naked round the room, treading repeatedly on the edge of the mattress. Surinder sat up on her elbows. For a while she watched me, narrow-eyed, one leg drawn towards her. Then she said, 'What are you up to exactly?'

I slammed the book on the wall. 'Swatting mosquitoes.'

'Aren't you overdoing it?'

'No.' I walked backwards, craning my neck at the ceiling.

She said, 'You'll probably come back as one now. With any luck someone'll squidge you.'

'They're bloodsuckers,' I said.

'So close the window, don't let them in.'

I leapt and caught one, smudging the wallpaper. The wings stuck to the book and I flicked at the mess with my fingernail. 'There's too many insects,' I said. 'This house is full of them.'

'Do some cleaning then.'

I tossed the book on the bed. 'Maybe.' The husks of last summer's flies lay in the dust on the window sill. I gathered them into my hand and leant out of the window. The air was damp and warm. Below me the grass and leaves appeared blue and the colours in Gran's flowers seemed darker, a shade deeper. The sun shone from behind thickening clouds. I tipped the flies from my palm and watched as they fell, spiralling down into nettles.

Surinder said, 'In India you know, there's insects everywhere. Only you don't pay any attention because there's so many. But if you get just one little fly in England it drives everyone nuts and they start whipping out the aerosols.'

'It's a book,' I said, turning round. 'Ozone friendly.'

She wiped its cover on the edge of the mattress, laid it on the floorboards. 'But just imagine if there were hundreds of flies, and ants everywhere, huge things like moths, and midges all over the place. You'd go crazy.'

'Who wouldn't?'

'But you don't notice. If there's flies everywhere you just let them get on with it. Like the heat, if it's hot all the time you stop bothering about it. You just roast away and put up with it.'

I lay down at her side. 'You've only ever been for

holidays,' I said. 'If you had to stay there forever you'd hate it. How long do you think you'd stick it for, really?'

Surinder straightened her legs on the mattress. Her skin made three folds on her stomach. I stroked my hand on her breast and felt the nipple become taut, dragging against my palm. She pushed me away. 'I don't know,' she said. 'But if I saw any mice in this place I'd probably freak, yet when we were over there we had lizards and mice and all sorts just crawling up the walls and we didn't think twice about it. There was a family of mice came out every evening. Did you know mice climb walls?'

'They do that everywhere,' I said. 'I saw one in the conservatory.' Surinder looked at me sharply and I smiled, locked my hands under my head. 'Ages ago,' I said.

'Have you ever seen a snake?'

'No. Plenty of worms though. Slugs, snails, frogs . . .'

'We had them. And cows, and donkeys . . .' She counted them off on her fingers. 'Snakes, bullocks, chickens, camels, all sorts – but especially mosquitoes. I tell you, I was covered in lumps.'

'Any pigs?' I asked her.

She nodded. 'There were these little pigs which just sort of ran around the place. They didn't belong to anyone, I think they just fed off the rubbish. Really noisy, but they ran away if you even looked at them. We didn't used to go near them because everyone thinks they're filthy. Dirty. Even when they're not.'

'That's Muslims,' I said.

'Yes, Danny. And Jews.' She pretended to yawn, patting a hand on her mouth. A warm wind blew from the quarries and rattled the window. The smell of our pig mingled with the stench from the tip. A seagull dipped into view, white against the darkening sky, and Surinder said, 'You know, most of my aunts would rather feed the birds than give anything to a pig. Pigs are so low in the hierarchy.'

'But they still eat them.'

'Yes.'

'What about cows?'

'They're top of the hierarchy.'

'Do they eat them?' I asked. She didn't reply. 'Surinder?'

'Some do,' she sighed, 'some don't. It's boring. Let's talk about something else.'

She rolled onto her front and I turned with her. We lay with our elbows splayed out, our chins resting on the backs of our hands. Against the skirting board Surinder's vase of flowers was surrounded by shrivelling petals. The heads of the flowers were bare and the leaves and stalks had turned to green mulch in the water. There was a condom in the dirt at the head of the mattress. I picked it up and shook it gently. The bulb of fluid had turned to grey. Surinder watched but didn't speak and when I smiled she lowered her eyelids. She had brought the condoms from her father's shop. She took them when he wasn't watching, slipped the money in the till later. Sometimes when he looked at her she started to blush, she thought he could see into her head.

She murmured, 'Put it down, Danny, it's really sordid.'

As I dropped the condom I caught a faint smell of rubber from my fingers. 'Tell me some more about India,' I said.

She lay one cheek on her hands and faced me. Her eyes were dark, unblinking, and when she spoke her voice was soft, almost a whisper. 'You know the house where we stayed, it was the house where I would've been born if my family hadn't come to England. That's where I would've grown up. I'd have scrubbed pots and pans with ashes and made up fires with cow dung. It's really hard work you know. The water and electricity kept going off, every couple of hours they went off at the mains. You felt like you were covered in dust all the time. That's what really got to me. Life is so full of hard work out there.'

'It's full of hard work here,' I said.

'Except that you don't bother doing it.' I shrugged and Surinder said, 'I wouldn't have known what one of those was either. No boyfriends or anything. I probably wouldn't even be allowed out, not like this, not where no one knows where I am.' Her bangle was pressing into the side of her face. She lifted her chin, gave a flick of her wrist.

'It's a good job you're here then.'

'Maybe,' she said, frowning. 'But it wouldn't have been so bad, you know. It's what you're used to, isn't it? We had fresh bullocks' milk every day, and yoghurt, and loads of fruit. And the women are more in charge there, they're much more respected, so you do what they tell you. There aren't so many macho men strutting about.'

'Like who?'

She raised herself on her elbows, eased the bangle from her hand. 'You, for instance.'

'I'm not a macho man.'

Surinder smiled. She circled the steel hoop through her fingers, rubbed the metal where it was dirty. 'I might've been married by now anyway.'

'To the fat creep?'

'Probably.' She held the bangle over one eye, looked at me through the hoop. 'But it might've been okay, you never know. Things might've seemed different. If I stayed with him for years and years I might've fallen in love with him. That's what's supposed to happen, after about a hundred years you don't mind if he's ugly.' She sat upright on the edge of the mattress, one foot beneath her, the other in the dust of the floorboards. She seemed self-conscious now, flicked the hair from her face, avoiding my eyes. 'Here,' she said, and tugged my arm from under me. She tried to slide

the bangle onto my hand, narrowing my fingers in hers.
But the hoop was too small and it wedged at my knuckles.

'I'll do it,' I said. I sat facing her. My hand was broad
and the bangle dug into the base of my thumb. I forced it
down by fractions, working one side and then the other,
using my fingernails to get under the metal. Surinder
watched me. 'What's it called?' I asked.

'*Kara.*' She sounded reluctant, sighed when she spoke.
'It's to protect the arm you hold your sword with.'

'Yeah?'

'It's meant to represent the oneness of God.' Her eyes
met mine and she smiled. 'Something like that.'

Suddenly the hoop slid free, hung loose round my wrist.
I sucked at the graze on my knuckle. 'The sword's called a
kirpan,' I said.

'Well done.'

'Tell me some more,' I said.

'About what?'

'Marriage for instance.'

Surinder stretched across to our clothes and dragged
them towards her. 'Some arranged marriages are okay,' she
said. 'Sometimes they work.' She pushed her arms in the
sleeves of her T-shirt, pulled it over her head. 'My brother
didn't want one, not to start with, but it's like a community
thing, that's what they all tell you – it brings everyone
together because the marriage is shared out, it isn't just one
couple. It's two families.' She separated the legs of her
jeans from mine. 'And he's happy now, he's glad he did it.'

The bangle was lighter than I imagined. I shook my arm
and admired it. Bluish stripes marked the back of my hand.
I said, 'Will you come and visit Grandad?'

Surinder slipped her jeans over her ankles, pulled them
to her hips as she stood. The air cooled, became darker.
She picked up her vase of flowers and crossed to the

window. 'Could do I suppose,' she said. The rain on the roof came sudden and heavy. She emptied the vase in the garden and closed the window. As she turned round she said, 'You'll never get that bangle off now. What if your grandad asks about it?'

'I'll tell him it's a *kara*, and it's supposed to protect your fighting arm, and it means the oneness of God.'

'What if he asks about me?'

'I'll say you gave me it.'

Surinder smiled. She stooped for her book and said, 'I'm going downstairs to read.'

'Wait.' I drew my jeans onto my lap and felt in the pockets. My fingers were trembling and when I found my grandmother's ring I fumbled and dropped it. It was cold and smooth. I placed it in the palm of my hand. 'Here.'

'What is it?'

'Gran's ring.'

She raised her eyes to meet mine, smiling, uncertain. Then she shook her head and said, 'No, Danny, you keep it.'

'It's a fair swap,' I said.

'I couldn't.'

'Why not?'

'I don't know, I just couldn't.'

I closed my fist over the ring and sighed, sank back to the mattress. Droplets were falling from a damp patch in the ceiling, splashing onto the floorboards. 'I can't figure you out,' I said. 'I never know what you're really thinking.'

There was a long pause and quietly she said, 'I don't know what I'm really thinking.' I waited, watching the rain, but she didn't say any more. I heard the door open and close, and listened to her footsteps as she descended the staircase. When the thunder broke overhead the mosquitoes separated, settled again in different positions. I saw them in the next flash of lightning.

TWENTY-FIVE

MY BROTHER said, 'That's for definite then. They're taking it?'

Rachael nodded, smiling. 'So Tom says.'

'Christ sake,' he said, and spat in the sink. He turned the tap with two twists of his hand and crouched to look in the cupboard below. His face reddened. The water drummed in the washing-up bowl and splashed back on the worktop and tiles. Mum leant across him to lower the pressure.

'Are you staying to eat, Rachael?' she said.

My sister parted her knees for Lucy and shook her head. 'Not tonight, Mum' she murmured, watching as Richard rummaged through the liquids and dishcloths. Suddenly he swept everything to the floor and picked out the nailbrush. He tossed it into the sink and bundled the rest of the things back on the shelf. When he began to scour his fingernails Rachael said, 'Dirty work then, Richard?'

'Beats sitting on your arse all day.'

'Grumpy Uncle Richard,' Rachael whispered, and Lucy twisted to hide in her mother's shoulder.

Outside the rain fell steadily. It gushed past the window from the overflow pipe, spattering the rubbish bin and the edge of the patio. In the watery light of the kitchen the face of the clock appeared green. It was half past five. My father turned the dial on his transistor radio, found a jingle for our local station and lowered the volume. Mum pulled an apron from the drawer. As she flapped out the folds she said, 'I was thinking, you know – your grandad was one of the first to settle in this town. You'd think that would give him some rights. He says he practically walked here. A lot of the men say that, the ones from Scotland. Don't they, Danny?'

I looked down, positioned myself in the centre of the doorway. My toes were on the kitchen linoleum, heels resting on the living room carpet. Behind me I could hear Katie flicking through the television channels. 'I wouldn't know,' I said.

'You'd think it would count for something,' Mum said, tying a knot in her apron strings. 'At one time it would've done.'

Rachael watched me from under her fringe, her nose buried in Lucy's hair. I raised my eyebrows, and she said, 'Have you decided about that pig yet, Danny?' I shrugged. She imitated me. 'What's that supposed to mean?'

'It means *Not really. No, I haven't really thought about it.*'

'He's away with the fairies,' my father said. 'Dreamland.' He laid his cigarette in a saucer and looked beneath his chair for his shoes. The coarse skin of his neck had been shaved at the barber's and there were scrape marks at the back of each ear. I watched as he placed his left shoe beside his left foot, stood the other on the table by his elbow. From the wall unit above he took down a blue shoebox and shook out a yellow cloth. He folded it once, draped it over his kneecap.

Mum said, 'Can that not wait till after dinner?'

'No,' he said, and took a drag on his cigarette. He tugged his brushes apart, exhaling brown smoke, and dabbed the bristles of the smaller brush into the polish. As he began to stroke the side of his shoe he said to my sister, 'You know, Rachael, I've worked with these people, and they're decent enough folk, you can share a pot of tea with them, but they don't belong. Tom should've taken that into account. The Council don't want to go mixing up the neighbourhoods.'

Rachael said quietly, 'Tom had nothing to do with it, Dad.'

'The Council, anyway,' my father said. 'Tom's employers.'

He examined the heel of his shoe, conscious that she was watching him. After a few moments Rachael turned away, shaking her head, and said to my mother. 'Since when have you wanted Grandad to live on this estate anyway?'

'Nothing wrong with the estate,' Mum said. She swept some potatoes into a saucepan. 'This has never been a bad place to live.'

'Until now,' Richard said.

'You've never heard me complain about the estate,' my mother said. She dipped her hands in the washing-up bowl and wiped her fingers in her apron. Easing Richard aside she took my swill tub from under the sink, lifted it quickly to the height of her chin. Her face tightened. 'This smells, Danny,' she said. 'It needs washing.' I didn't reply and she threw the tub back in the cupboard, slammed the door shut with her knee. As she dropped a handful of peelings into the pedal bin she said, 'Your responsibility, not mine.' I nodded. She picked up a knife and held it poised above the chopping board. Her face and neck were pink. The radio crackled. Suddenly she turned and shouted, 'Do you hear me!'

'Yes,' I said. Dad's brush scuffed back and forth on his shoe. In the living room I could hear the test match. Something exciting was happening, the crowd cheering and the commentators laughing. I craned my neck and saw the light cast from the screen to the opposite wall, Katie sitting high on the sofa, staring back at it.

Dad rested his shoe on his knee, suppressing a smile. 'There's one thing about this business anyway, Danny,' he said. 'You don't want our new neighbours to know what you get up to all day. Pig man. They wouldn't like that. Oh, *jabber jabber jabber*.' He put on an Indian accent, tilting his head from side to side. 'Sacred animal,' he explained. 'They wouldn't like that.'

'It's not sacred,' I told him. 'It's the opposite.' But he wasn't listening. He placed his brush to one side and picked up the cloth, began to buff the toe of his shoe. As the last of the water drained from the sink Richard leant back on the worktop. He flicked the wet from his hands.

'I reckon that pig's had it,' he said, smiling. 'It's on its way out. What do you think, Danny?' I made no response, but watched him. In recent days the pig had become slower each morning to emerge from her shelter, seemed tired and listless, unable to eat all the food in her trough. I had not told this to Richard; I did not see how he could know. Still smiling, he said to my father, 'I've told him. If he wants a price for his pig then Craig'll sort it. But if he leaves it too long it'll be too late. They'll be demolishing all that area before long. House, garden, the lot. The park will be massive when it's up and running.' He reached across and switched on the strip light. The tube buzzed and flickered. 'They might even give you a job, Danny. They'll be wanting folk to dress up at some point – period costume and all that.'

I said, 'All *what* exactly?' but he grinned and didn't answer, folded his arms on his chest.

At the cooker Mum struck a match, and then another, almost dropping the box. The matches were damp and wouldn't light and she threw the box at the window ledge, into a pool of water. The frame was leaking. She clicked her tongue and snatched up my father's lighter. She had to shake it several times and when finally the gas rings were ignited she stood watching the flames, her arms tense at her sides. I felt a movement and glanced down. Katie had eased herself into the doorway beside me. She took hold of my bangle and tried to force it over my wrist. 'It's a shame,' Mum said then. 'They used to keep that garden lovely at one time.'

'The garden's not too bad now,' Richard said. 'All he needs is a girl out there to help with the housework.'

'He had better not,' Mum said. She looked around for my father's cigarettes. 'Are you listening, Danny?'

I shrugged, and Katie said, 'You're wearing a bracelet!'

'It's a bangle,' I told her. 'Not a bracelet.' I tugged my arm upwards and she laughed, collapsing her weight. She hung on with both hands.

My mother glanced at my wrist, holding a fresh cigarette in the tips of two fingers. 'And that had better not be your grandmother's,' she said.

My sister sighed heavily. Her face was flushed and the hair was damp on her forehead. She licked the pad of her thumb and smeared it around Lucy's mouth. 'Play with Katie now,' she whispered, and slumped back in the chair. For several seconds the girls faced each other across the kitchen, my father sitting between them, then Katie stamped a foot and her sister screeched, suddenly ducked under the table. Dad caught his polish before it fell to the floor. He took a long intake of breath, raising his eyebrows at Rachael. The girls were giggling. Rachael said, 'Could you open a window please, Mum?'

'It's raining.'

'Very stuffy though.'

Reluctantly my mother put down her cigarette. She unlocked the back door and pushed it ajar on its chain. The garden outside was dark. As the noise of the rain increased my father turned a dial on his radio. He dropped his shoes to the floor and pulled them over his feet, carefully fastened the laces. He peered into the shine on his toecaps. Pointing out at the rain Mum said, 'You know, Rachael, there hasn't been anyone in that bungalow for years. Years that's been empty. It was meant for the old folks in the beginning, wasn't it? So you'd think they'd let an old couple have it now, someone local. But this couple aren't even old, apart from anything else. From what I saw they were a very young couple.'

'Any old person will do then?' Rachael said, waving a hand through Mum's smoke. 'It doesn't have to be Grandad?'

My mother picked up a packet of sausages from the worktop and pierced the wrapping with her thumbnail. She tore it open. 'Whether it's your grandad or not, Rachael, that bungalow was meant for the old folks. But now the Council has other ideas. As soon as they get these Pakistanis on the housing list they won't entertain us, suddenly they aren't interested.' She pricked each of the sausages with her knife, dropped them into a frying pan.

'You may be right,' Rachael sighed. 'I'm not arguing.'

Richard took a drag on my mother's cigarette. He smiled

to himself, looking down at the girls. I followed his gaze. A yellow puddle had formed around Lucy's sandals. She was crouching with her skirt pulled back from her knees. Katie came out from under the table and stood beside me at the door. She looked up to my face and I said, 'Lucy's wet herself, Rachael.'

My mother glanced down and groaned. She pushed Richard aside, took a bucket and mop from the pantry. As she rinsed the mop at the sink she said, 'I suppose we'll be getting all the smells when they move next door.'

'Same smells as anyone else,' Rachael said sharply. She dragged Lucy to her feet. 'Upstairs,' she murmured.

I stepped backwards into the living room, stood where I could see the television. As Katie hurried behind Rachael my mother called after them, 'Mind she doesn't drip on the carpet!' and shook her head is if expelling a bad taste.

'Is Rachael getting any dinner?' my father said then.

'No,' Mum said.

Dad looked at Richard, raising his eyebrows. 'Was she asked?'

'Yes,' said Mum, and swept a damp mop across the linoleum, splashing the polished toes of his shoes. Richard pulled the door closed behind him and lay down on the sofa. As my parents began to shout in the kitchen he said, 'So what's with the bracelet, Danny?'

I looked away from the television to the rain streaking the window. 'It means the oneness of God,' I said.

TWENTY-SIX

THE FOYER of the old people's home was lit by high windows on three sides and cluttered with pot-plants and flowers. A metal trolley sat empty outside a room labelled *Private*. Double firedoors gave on to the main lounge, and on our right there was a corridor, a row of dark panelled doors leading down to the laundry and kitchens. The first of these doors was open to the Matron's office. She stood near her desk, gazing down at her telephone. One hand was pushed back through her hair. When she saw us she waved, and Surinder hesitated. 'Does she want to talk to us?' she whispered.

The lift was engaged. 'I doubt it,' I said, and we began climbing the stairs as the telephone started to ring.

In the second-floor lounge the carpeting was a different colour and there was a birdcage next to the television. Tall windows gave a view of the carpark and a terrace of houses on the other side of the road. Our bicycles were propped against the janitor's bungalow. Shaded from the sun by a wicker screen the old people sat in the same positions as on every other day. Most of them were women and several were knitting. As we passed between their chairs one old lady said, 'You needn't bring that darkie near me,' and watched us nervously, her blue eyes like buttons. I took Surinder's hand in mine and led her past an upright piano, a shuttered bar, and along the wide corridor to my grandfather's room. Her palm was clammy and she tugged herself free when we arrived at his door. I knocked twice. Grandad was sitting on the edge of his bed, folding his handkerchief and gazing at space. As I led Surinder into the room he seemed for a moment confused, as if suddenly wakened. I said, 'This is Surinder, Grandad.'

His face was unshaven. He nodded uncertainly.

'She's been helping me at the cottage, looking after the pig.'

'The pig? Oh aye.'

'And in the garden,' she said.

'Very good.' He watched as I sat down and then indicated his wheelchair to Surinder. 'Have a seat, dear,' he said. He pushed the handkerchief into his pocket and glanced at his cigarettes. Then he clasped his hands in his lap.

'Would you like a drink, Grandad?' I said, and placed the cigarette packet on the bedspread beside him.

'Aye, son. Aye.'

'Whisky?'

'I'll take a can today, son,' he said.

He nodded as I opened the door of his bedside cabinet, and leant a little towards me, as if expecting something to fall out. When I gave him the beer can he struggled to slip his fingernail under the ring-pull. Surinder said, 'Shall I do it?' and sat forward in the wheelchair. But he returned the can to me and waited as I opened and poured it. Surinder remained sitting forwards, her hands between her knees, and looked around at his room.

The only sound then was the fizz of the beer, the regular clicks of Grandad's alarm clock. He brought the glass to his lips and swallowed, wiped the back of his hand on his mouth. He glanced at Surinder as she examined his room, and drank again. Finally he said, 'I've just the one can, dear, but will you take a wee nip?' He nodded to his whisky bottle.

I caught Surinder's eye and she said, 'Yes.' Then, 'Thank you.'

He lit a cigarette as I poured out two whiskies. We each said, 'Cheers.' I noticed his hair was uncombed, the bed-clothes ruffled behind him. He took several short breaths on his cigarette and when he was sure it was burning he turned and looked at Surinder. Finally he said, 'So the beast's behaving itself?'

Surinder spoke clearly and loudly. 'Yes,' she said, 'she's been very good.'

'Because she can be a crabbit old bastard ye know. If she doesnae get her grub.' He winked at me. 'That right, son? The old folks get awfy crabbit if they dinnae get their grub.'

'That's right.'

'Aye.' For some time then he was quiet, gazing inwards, not drinking or smoking. Surinder lifted an eyebrow and I shrugged, replaced my small glass on the cabinet. Surinder brought hers to her lips, drank a little and coughed. I picked up my grandfather's watch and began to rewind it. He frowned as he turned to Surinder. 'I mind the first time I ever set eyes on a pig, dear,' he said. 'I saw it slaughtered. It's a sight ye cannae forget. It was a December, ye know, and my father, he used tae lend a hand in the slaughterhouse there. That was the slaughterhouse where my wife's father worked.' Grandad took a mouthful of beer and drew on his cigarette. 'Have I told ye this one, son?'

'No,' I said. I was listening.

'Well, my father smoked a wee clay pipe, and he smoked it as he walked along tae his work – it was casual labour, he wasnae a slaughterman himself – and this particular night I tagged along behind him. I mind it was awfy cold and there was a layer of snow on the ground and I was walking along in his boot treads. The air turned tae vapour as ye breathed, and I pretended I had a pipe too.' He brought his cigarette to his mouth and sucked at the air, blowing imaginary smoke. 'But when we got tae the slaughterhouse he looked back and saw me and he shooed me away, like ye would a dog, because he didnae want me inside, d'ye see. He didnae want me tae see what went on. So I went around the back.

'Well, there were some other boys there, mostly weans, and I elbowed my way up for a better view. We were standing on a high wall, leaning up tae the windows – and they were awfy filthy windows, grimy, with smuts of midges from the summer. It was lit by a gas mantle inside. And there was my father, backing in through the door – he was coming backwards, shuffling along, d'ye see? There was a gutter along the middle of the floor and he had his feet on either side of this gutter. He was pulling a rope, leaning backwards, and on the end of the rope was this pig, the first one I saw. But when the pig had its head through the door it decided that was enough, it widnae go any further, it stiffened its legs and it widnae move another inch. It was feart, pet.' Grandad lowered his voice and leaned towards Surinder. 'It was squealing. Terrified, d'ye see?' He was frowning. Surinder nodded.

'Well, Agnes's old man – that was my wife's name, pet –

he stood just inside the doorway. He had the pig just where he wanted it, that suited him. They wore breeches and buskins then, and an oilskin apron, and he had forearms like hams. He was a big brute of a man, red-haired ye know, red hairs all down his arms. And he had a poleaxe. Well, he smote the pig on the back of the head and it just slumped down in the gutter. One hit, and down it went. But it wisnae dead. He was a very skilled man, ye understand. He stunned it, he held this hammer like a punch and he knocked it unconscious. Because he wanted the heart tae keep going, tae pump all the blood out when he cut the throat – because you used that for black pudding. Blood and oatmeal.' He licked his lips and Surinder smiled.

'They sliced the throat anyway,' he told her, 'and they pumped the blood intae this basin. My father and this other man, they pressed down on the pig with their feet and lifted the forelegs up and down like a pump. And Agnes's mother, she was in there as well – she was wearing a man's cap, like Agnes herself used to, and a black shawl – she stirred the blood around in the basin. She was only a wee woman, four feet nothing – a tiny wee soul – and she had a face on her like a mouthful of lemons. Awfy bitter-looking woman. Coarse as a horse too, she wisnae afraid tae speak out, she aye spoke her mind.

'Now, with a pig ye want tae scrape it as soon as ye can, plenty of hot water. And I mind my father and this other wee fella, they carried the water, steaming coppers of water which they poured in a tub. They lifted the pig by its four legs – hup! – and they lowered it into the water. It would've been dead by now, pet. And then they all knelt down and scraped away the hairs. Blunt knives, ye know. Because ye wouldnae want tae cut the skin. Well, I mind the windows were getting awfy steamed up at this point, and some of the other boys, they lost interest, or made way and let the next ones up – but I stood my ground. I had an idea what was coming next. I could see a rope and pulley attached to the ceiling, and right enough they used that for the pig, hoisted it up by the hind legs. And Agnes's father, he took a sharp knife and he slit the beast right down the middle.' Grandad turned to me. 'You put a finger each side of the blade, son, and you cut and pull, cut and pull. There's a wee fold of fat and skin which ye have tae pull apart. Then my father and this other fella, they held a pan to the gash and Agnes's father, he reached inside and give a wee tug and all the guts came out, tumbled out – they were grey, disgusting sight. And then he tossed a bag of shit against the far wall, a big ball of shit.' He started to laugh, and then said, 'Sorry dear.'

Surinder grinned, shaking her head.

'Well, there was an art tae that too. The lungs and the heart were taken out separately and they were laid on a slab bench. Agnes's mother, she washed all that down. Then the head was cut behind the back bone on either side, cut away, and that's what my father took home. He took a few coppers for his trouble, no a lot, and this head wrapped up in a newspaper. I followed him. I was looking for the blood to drip in the snow, but it was all drained off. All gone.' Grandad's cigarette had burned to the stub and I passed him an ashtray. He lit another, and said, 'You used tae get quite a lot off a pig's head in those days. You tied the brain in a muslin bag, if ye didnae mind eating brain – that was very tasty on toast, looks like soft roe.'

Grandad nodded, and Surinder asked him, 'Did you used to slaughter your own pigs?'

'We didnae kill our own, no.' He reached to touch her arm. 'Because ye see, Agnes had seen enough of that, and she didn't fancy it – all the work – so we used to send ours away. There was a farmer came and collected them.'

'Ted,' said Surinder.

'Aye, Ted.' My grandfather looked at her in surprise, as if he had forgotten the name. 'It was Ted, aye. But he'll be dead by now. He was old when I knew him. It was his sons took over, they used tae come instead.' He said to me, 'Your gran could never get on with them, Danny. The boys. She relied on Ted, ye know, he was very obliging. Because ye see, Agnes was an awfy superstitious soul. Your folk are a wee bit that way, are they no, pet? The things ye can and cannae do where grub is concerned. Agnes now, she would never have a pig killed on a Friday, she said that was very bad luck. And if ye had the beast slaughtered when the moon was on the wane, well that meant the meat wouldnae keep. And something else again when it was a full moon. There were others besides. I cannae mind them all, but Ted – he knew, and he fell in with whatever Agnes wanted. And I mind we used tae use every last scrap of the animal, nothing was wasted. Only thing ye couldnae eat was the squeal! That's an old saying.'

'The pig was important,' Surinder said. She sipped the last of her whisky.

'It was, aye, it was important. Because this is the thing – we used tae buy a new pig every Hogmanay, and then we spent the following year fattening that up on scraps before we killed it the following Christmas. And that was important, it was a neighbourly thing, everything was shared out. We took the scraps in from the neighbours, and we passed them a wee joint of meat when it came back from the butcher. D'ye see, ye had tae get on with folk. And sometimes we kept more than one pig, but they never went short of grub. There was always someone chapping the door with a scrap of something for the pot. I mind we had four pigs one year, raised them all up and sold them. That was the year Richard was born, Danny's brother. Have ye met his brother, pet?'

'I've seen him,' she said.

'Aye.' Grandad held out his hand for his watch, twisted it onto his wrist. 'Aye. Richard. I cannae mind when I last saw him. I don't see much of him now.'

'Danny said you might move to the bungalow next door, on the estate.'

My grandfather's face darkened, and he said, 'Aye, well, they might want me to move next door, pet. But no me. I've no desire tae move.'

'You're happy here,' Surinder said.

For a long time my grandfather was silent, and when finally he replied he spoke to me. 'The fact is this, d'ye see son, I've nae heart left. I'm an old man now, and I've nae heart. That's away with your gran. This is what I'm saying. Agnes is away now and all I need is provided here. So there's nae sense in moving me.'

'No,' I said.

'This is where I belong now,' he said.

'Yes.'

He picked up his whisky bottle and said to Surinder, 'Will ye take another, pet?' but she placed a hand over her glass.

'I'll have to go soon,' she said.

'Aye,' he said. 'But you'll maybe come again.'

Surinder smiled but didn't reply. My grandfather gave me his empty beer glass. 'Any more in that can, son?'

I turned it upside down. 'All gone,' I said.

TWENTY-SEVEN

MY GRANDMOTHER's basket was hanging from a beam in the roof of the conservatory. A ribbon of cobweb clung to my fingers when I tried to remove it. Inside I found a few crumbs of grey soil, some dried and shrivelled leaves. On the bench-top a pair of garden cutters sat next to the grinding-wheel. I picked them up and saw a spider scurrying for cover, another following. I dropped the cutters in the basket and slipped one of Gran's knives into my pocket, swept the spiders to the floor. Outside Surinder was waiting at the bean trellis, her hands deep in the pockets of Gran's raincoat. A wind blew through the leaves of the apple trees and whipped in her hair. 'Cold?' I called.

She nodded, half shrugged. I set the basket on the ground and gave her the cutters. 'What will you use?' she said.

'This.' I unfolded the blade from its handle. 'Grandad made it. He's got his initials in the wood.' But as I held up the knife Surinder reached into the bush, crouching away from me. She clipped the stem of a bean pod. I said, 'You okay with the cutters then?'

Her voice was muffled. 'Yes.'

For some time we worked without speaking, the trellis creaking in the wind, leaves rustling. In the distance a mechanical digger was reducing an earth-pile, loading rubble onto the back of a truck. A second lorry was driving away from them. Briefly a couple of men in yellow helmets appeared at the crest of a rise, carrying rods and clipboards. I stopped for a moment to watch them. Surinder poured a handful of pods into the basket and walked to the other side of the bush. I said through the foliage, 'Mum's been up the Council offices, you know. About the bungalow.'

She worked slowly, reaching upwards. 'Yeah?'

'She wore her best clothes and everything. Took the day off work.' I lifted my voice above the wind. 'She needed to as well – they kept her waiting for hours. Then she reckons they just ignored everything she said, so now she's raging. She says she's going to get a petition up.'

After a pause Surinder asked, 'What did she say to them?'

'Just about the bungalow.'

'Like?'

'Well, she claims it was only meant for old folks – that's why it was built in the first place – and the Council promised it to Grandad.'

'But she doesn't want him to live there.'

I took a breath. 'She didn't, but now she says it's the principle of the thing. And she wants to know what happened to Council waiting lists . . . All that sort of stuff.'

Surinder appeared at my side. She emptied a pocket of bean pods. 'So what's her petition about?'

'She hasn't done it yet.'

'But?'

'Something about the people who live on the estate having the right to say who moves in. That was one. Or else, only old people who've been in the town for so many years can get one of the bungalows.'

'Your mum's an old cow,' Surinder said.

With a shrug I said, 'Suppose so.' I looked down at the pod in my hand, ran my thumb over its surface, the clear outline of the beans inside. As I tossed it to the basket I said, 'Gran used to save the seeds, you know. For planting next year.'

Surinder allowed her cutters to fall to the soil. 'I know.'

'I don't think I'll bother,' I said.

She nodded, tucked her hair inside the raincoat. 'I'm going to look at Agnes,' she said. She picked a way through the nettles that surrounded us and strolled past the vegetables, her head down, brushing the leaves of the plants as she passed them. At the wall of the sty she stood on tip-toe and leaned forwards. Beside me the bush was still heavy with pods. After several minutes I left the basket and followed her.

At one time there had been clear footpaths through the allotment, narrow tracks of flattened soil, now covered with grasses and weeds. Wooden planks had been laid between the potato patch and the other vegetables. They were trodden into the earth, barely noticeable, but in places still sounded or gave under pressure. As a boy I had found the noisiest point in the gap between the two longest boards and there I used to jump up and down, shouting for my grandmother to watch me. Often she had shooed me away in annoyance.

I paused at this point now, flexing my weight on the wood and gazing down at the potatoes. The leaves of some of the plants had already withered, turned yellow by the rain. I kicked away the soil and found several tubers were rotten, crawling with grubs and insects. Behind me there was a row of shallots. I had pulled them a fortnight before, left them to dry in the sun. Now the leaves were brown slithers and soon they too would be wasted. Surinder called softly to the pig. I took a cluster of shallots and sliced away the stem with my knife.

She was staring towards the pig's shelter, her chin propped on one fist. I nudged her elbow with mine and held out my hand. 'Want one?'

'Onions?'

'Shallots.' She shook her head, and I said, 'Gran used to keep a few of these too. We could replant them if you like.'

'Now?'

'They go in next spring. February maybe.'

She gave a brief nod. Quietly she said, 'Are you sure the garden will be here in February, Danny?'

'I don't see why not.' I separated the bulbs, aimed one at the football in the corner of the sty.

'Do you think Agnes will be?'

'Yes,' I shrugged. 'Why shouldn't she?'

'She looks a bit done in to me.'

I fired another bulb at the football. 'She'll perk up,' I said. The shallot hit the wall and spun across the floor of the pen. We heard a rustle from the pig's shelter, a low grunting. She emerged shakily, damp grass on her back. Some dung had dried in the hairs of her hind legs. Before approaching the bulb she sniffed at the air, lifting her snout, her ears half-cocked. I said, 'I ought to take another look at her bedding.'

'Why don't you just call out a vet?'

I shrugged. 'We're probably not even supposed to have her.'

'Have you told your grandad she's ill?'

'I didn't want to worry him,' I said. Then added, 'He'd like to see you again, you know – he keeps asking after you, when you'll be coming up. He always gets your name wrong, though – he calls you Selina, or Sabrina.'

I was smiling. Surinder said, 'Why did you tell me that?'

'What?'

'It's like saying, he can't pronounce your paki name. Ha ha.'

'Surinder!'

She sighed heavily and turned away from me, staring out at the garden. After a moment she leant back on the breeze-block and folded her arms on her chest. 'Sorry,' she said. A wisp of hair blew over her face. She pushed it up with her fingers. 'He was nice, your grandad,' she said. 'It's a shame for him.'

'How is it?'

'Being cooped up all day, missing your gran and everything.'

'He's okay.'

'He's not okay, Danny. He's really lonely. You just won't face up to things. Just because he's in a home full of other lonely old people he's supposed to be okay? It was really awful in there.'

I clambered onto the wall of the sty. 'He likes the food anyway,' I said, 'and he gets looked after. They wash all his clothes for him, make his bed and everything. They wheel him downstairs to the bar every night.' I dropped inside the pen. The pig drank from her sink. 'And you heard him yourself, he doesn't want to be moved.'

'But he's still lonely.'

'He's okay,' I said.

'That room was so bare, Danny.'

'But there's nowhere else for him to go.'

'Because the pakis got his bungalow, I suppose.'

'No!'

The loudness of my voice surprised me. For some minutes there was silence between us. Strips of tinfoil clattered amongst the vegetables, and I waited, not speaking. Finally she said, 'I don't see why he can't live in your house, Danny. How is it okay to stay in that awful place full of senile old women but it's not okay to live with his own family?'

I sighed. 'But they don't want him, Surinder. It'd be even worse. There isn't a family any more, not really, all they ever do is argue. He'd hate it.'

'This country makes me sick,' she said.

'What's that got to do with it?'

Surinder shook her head, turned her face to the quarries. Moments later she pushed herself from the wall and walked away to the apple trees. She turned up the collar of Gran's raincoat and bent into the wind, hunching her shoulders. Behind me the pig was standing quite still at her trough. Her snout was wet, dripping water. I threw the remaining shallots at a dungheap and ducked into her shelter.

When we had spread the last of the pig's straw a fortnight before I had mixed it with grass freshly raked from the lawn. The lawnmower still stood in front of the house, the remaining grass too thick to cut, and the pig's bed had since become damp and mulchy, shrunken now, and darker, smelling sour. I thought of lifting it whole and dropping it over the side of the wall, but then she would have no bedding at all. Instead I pushed it outside with my foot, began to separate the dry grass from the wet. The flies which had been swirling above the dungheaps stretched out towards me and the pig retreated back to her shelter, settled herself on the concrete. When finally the grass began to scatter on the wind I lifted a bundle and carried it down to the greenhouse, leaving the gate unlatched behind me.

The first of the rain hit the glass panes as I opened the door. Inside the air was moistureless. Gran's tomato plants had shrivelled in their pots, the leaves brittle and falling away. I dropped the bundle on the floor and shuffled my feet, spreading it flat. Perhaps it would dry when the weather improved. I stood with my hands on my hips. In the corner beside me there was a stack of wooden crates, some plastic pots, a few unopened seed packets. I saw a faded illustration of spinach. The instructions on the back of the packet said to sow thinly in narrow drills. I tipped the contents into my palm and pushed the seeds around with a finger, looking out at Surinder.

She was walking amongst the trees and tall weeds at the farthest edge of the garden. I could see the pink flowers of willowherb, purple thistles, a few heads of cow parsley. The branches of the apple trees thrashed in the wind. Grey clouds streaked above them. For some minutes I watched her, trying to picture my grandmother, the shape she used to make in the trees. It was a part of her garden she had abandoned before I was born. Hidden amongst the weeds were the remains of some chicken coops, a bench where she used to sit with my grandfather in summer. Sometimes I had seen her looking down at the railway cutting, or across to the earth-piles, a basket of fruit hooked over her arm. From a distance she appeared remote, closed into herself, but would smile as I approached her. She often asked, 'What can you tell me?' Other times she said nothing, and it was her silence I remembered, standing beside her.

If I approached Surinder now I imagined she too would smile, and we could stand together, watch the rain coming in from the quarries. I glanced around for a margarine tub and poured my seeds carefully inside. But when I looked up

Surinder had gone. She was retracing her steps through the weeds, moving quickly, as if being chased. I rapped my knuckles on the window and waved. She lifted her knees, trying to run, and almost stumbled. As I came outside I picked up a spade.

'It's a rat, I just saw it!'

'Where?'

'In there. It's huge. Great big tail like this, I thought it was a snake.'

I flattened some nettles with the back of the shovel, treading forwards.

'What are you doing to do?'

'Hammer it.'

'It's probably just come up from the tip, Danny. Forget it.'

But I swiped at the nettles, ducking as they flew up around me. 'It's okay,' I said. 'I'll sort it.'

'Danny!' she shouted. 'Just leave it!'

She was almost in tears, furious with me. Breathlessly I said, 'If I don't get it they'll breed. By next year they'll be everywhere.'

'Who cares!'

'I do!'

I let the spade rest on my shoulder and faced her. The rain fell steadily between us. Away in the distance the men in yellow helmets were hurrying for cover. At the top of the garden the pig had emerged from her pen. She was standing quite still, bracing herself in the wind. 'Pig's out,' I said finally. 'I'd better get her in.'

'Fuck's sake, Danny.' I did not move. The rain mottled Surinder's raincoat, dripped down from her hair. She was crying. Very quietly she said, 'It's pointless, Danny,' and I dropped the spade in the weeds, watched as she returned to the cottage.

TWENTY-EIGHT

BEFORE BREAKFAST each morning I left our house for the cottage, taking food for the day, a few cigarettes from my mother's handbag. I cycled out as the mist rose from the fields, the air warm on my arms and the roads almost empty. Each evening I remained a little longer, came home under reddening skies. For several days I did not see Surinder. One afternoon I picked up a book she had left, a novel, and for an hour I read without pausing. Then I put it aside, face down on the fireplace tiles, and switched on the television. Later I copied some sentences from my history textbook, but soon became bored. For most of the time I sat and watched cricket, or spent long hours asleep on the mattress upstairs. I closed all the curtains and avoided the garden. I didn't do any housework. At lunch-times, when I went to visit my grandfather, I left the back door unlocked and a note on the table in case Surinder came round. *Back soon,* it said. *Grandad's ill.*

A doctor had been to examine him. 'Your grandad's taken a wee turn,' the Matron told me. 'But he'll be fine, no worries.' Then to Grandad she shouted, 'You'll have to go easy on the fags and booze now, Joe. And no more chasing loose women!' His eyes went wide and he laughed, but then he started to cough and could not stop. I ran some water from the tap in the corner. The Matron held the glass to his lips and circled a hand on his back, her skirt tightening over her hips. For three days afterwards he lay against a pile of pillows, covered to the waist with a candlewick bedspread. He drifted in and out of sleep, didn't expect to see my face when he woke, and nodded when he recognized me. He could not think of a name for Surinder, but asked instead, 'How's your pal keeping, Danny?' I pretended she was working in the garden, taking care of the pig. He smiled as he lowered his eyelids. I rewound his watch and glanced through his newspaper, waited until I had stayed for an hour. The curtains were closed against the sunlight, blocking the view to the cemetery.

On the Friday morning, as I was guiding Gran's bike from our gate, I met my father coming home from his night-shift. He said, 'Off to the farm then, Danny?' and smiled as he approached me. I nodded. He was cradling a bag of bread rolls, his cap and a paper under his arm. 'Not fancy a roll?' he said. 'Fried egg?'

I mounted the bicycle. 'No, thanks.'

He inclined his head to the house. 'Mum up yet?'

'Not yet.'

'Richard?'

'I think I heard him.'

My father held open the gate, squinted up to the bedroom windows. His tie was draped round his shoulders and his jacket unbuttoned. He seemed reluctant to go in. Soon Mum would waken and begin again on her housework. She called it spring cleaning and she started as soon as she rose in the mornings, then when she returned from the factory at tea-time. She had cleaned all the windows and washed and ironed the curtains, rearranged her ornaments to face into the square. She worked furiously, speaking only if we got in her way. She would not let anyone help her. In the evenings I left my shoes on the back doorstep and washed my hands before I entered the living room. The house smelled of air freshener and polish.

'Is the pig keeping okay?' Dad asked me.

'Not bad,' I shrugged.

'Still off her food?' he said.

'She's fine.'

He waited, expecting more, but I placed a foot on one pedal, ready to leave. The names of Spider and Stan were sprayed across the fence slats behind him. The graffiti was new. Dad pointed his thumb at the house. 'I'd better get in.'

'Yes,' I said.

He nodded. 'Right you are then, son. Don't work too hard.'

'No,' I said. And he watched as I cycled away from him.

The pig had not eaten since I last saw Surinder. When I arrived at the cottage she was lying on her side in the entrance to her shelter. She grunted softly as the garden gate swung on its hinge, turned her eyes when I spoke to her. I laid the bike against the wall of the sty and walked around to her trough. The swill which I'd poured the previous evening had developed a skin, smelled sourly like vomit. 'I'll get you some breakfast,' I said. But it was some minutes before I went down to the kitchen.

Already there were people working at the earth ridges,

men in hardhats and vests, others with jackets. From a distance it was hard to see what they were doing. There was no machinery, no noise except the gulls sweeping above them, a faint murmur of voices. I rested my arms on the wall. The stench from the sty was stronger than I had known it and the pig's dung mostly liquid. In one corner of the garden, close to the tip, I could see the dungpile which Gran had kept for her allotment. It sloped down from the top of the wall and continued into the surrounding nettles and grass. It was coated in dew. Gran had not liked it to be visible, always forked it into the soil before adding more. I had started a second pile beneath one of the apple trees. A haze of midges now hovered above it.

In the kitchen the curtains were drawn and the light was orange and murky. I struck a match to the gas beneath the swill pot, took a cigarette from my shirt pocket and held it into the flames. My notebook still lay on the table. When the cigarette started to burn I pulled out a chair and picked up my pencil, opened a fresh page. The first of the smoke made my head spin. I closed my eyes and sat back, remembered the grass bank on the day of Gran's funeral, Surinder sitting above me and the sun shimmering behind her. There had been a carrier bag of library books beside us. I rested my chin in my hand and wrote, *Dear Surinder*. I supposed she would be at the library now.

In case you come round I've gone to see Grandad – he's not been very well – a bit of a cold – but getting better now. He asks after you quite often – seems he'd still like to see you again! So would Agnes by the way, and me (I won't be gone long). As I drew on the cigarette and stared at my notebook I pictured Surinder wading through the brook at the foot of the slope, her legs breaking the sheen of oil on the surface. I had trailed behind her, the impression of her body lingering against me, becoming cool in the sunlight. The water smelled, and she had hugged herself because it was cold. I remembered the dandelion she had wound round her finger and tried to recall what she had said to me.

No point in asking where you've been but I've been thinking I'll probably give school a miss now, I don't know but I don't see the point any more, not for me. I might try and stick it out here in the cottage – move in properly and get a job somewhere, maybe even LeisureLand. I don't think I can stand it at home anyway (looks like the petition has fallen through by the way – Mum is going mad with the duster etc.) Maybe you could still come and visit – if you want to? There'll always be pig shit to clean up. I think I might try and breed them after all, do it seriously and get registered and all that. The swill was beginning to bubble on the stove. I ground the cigarette under my foot and stood to light another. Before I sat down I eased my grandmother's ring from my pocket, placed it on the table beside my notebook. I wrote, *I still want to give you Gran's ring. I'd like you to keep it. You could maybe put it on a chain or something, then no one would have to see it – it's up to you but I would like you to have it.* I rose again. There was more to write, and I stood for some time looking down at the page, the grey pencilled words, saying in my head what I could not add. I bent to lift a metal pail from under the sink, filled it with water and tucked a tea-towel into my belt. I went outside.

There was a shovel propped against the side of the cottage in the sunlight. I laid it on my shoulder and carried it up to the sty. The bucket splashed water onto my shoes, clanked when I set it down on the concrete. The pig pricked her ears and watched me, but she did not attempt to get up. From somewhere close by I heard two men talking. They were descending into the railway cutting. One wore a tweed jacket, a bright yellow vest above it, and a pair of green wellingtons. I thought I recognized him from earlier in the week, one of the surveyors perhaps, but now the men were carrying no instruments. When they disappeared from view I turned and shovelled the old swill from the trough, dumped the mess over the wall.

I scoured the inside of the trough with a scrubbing brush and wiped it all down with the tea-towel. The remaining swill was like porridge and I emptied the water on top of it, sluiced it out with my hand. I rinsed the towel and took it down to the litter bin, held my breath against the smell when I lifted the lid. As I stood facing the empty space of the steel site I heard the men's voices becoming more distant. They appeared to be following the line of the track, walking away from the cottage. In the kitchen the next pot of feed was simmering on the stove. I supposed it would be ready when I had finished clearing the sty. I went across to the greenhouse for the wheelbarrow.

When finally I brought the fresh swill from the kitchen my jeans and shirt were smeared with dung. A thick layer of dirt caked my shoes and made them appear several sizes larger. As I walked I looked down at them and smiled. I was glad to be dirty. There were dark marks on my nose, dung splashes in my hair. The pig coughed when she saw me. I crouched at her side and stroked her ears and snout, gently encouraged her to stand. Her body trembled as she rose and I noticed that her knees were swollen. She walked into the sunlight, breathing harshly, but when she began to eat she appeared contented. She did not hear the men's voices. They emerged from the cutting at the rear of the garden and walked around the back of the cottage. As they strolled amongst the piles of rubble in the neighbouring plots I looked at the man in the yellow vest and realized it was the farmer who had driven the Land-Rover.

I went and stood at the hedge beyond Gran's roses. The men spoke quietly to each other as they walked, looking down at the ground, their voices muffled, indistinct. The second man was younger and when he stooped to lift an old boot from the grass his fringe fell over his eyes. He flicked his head, and tossed the boot away. The farmer glanced to see where it landed. There was surprise on his face when he noticed me. He raised his eyebrows further and smiled. I said, 'What are you doing?'

'I'm sorry?'

He stepped through the long weeds towards me, the other man following. I squinted into the sun. 'I was just wondering what you were doing.'

'Cogitating,' he said, and widened his smile. His face was broad and tanned, pockmarked on the cheeks. Standing before me the men appeared very large, their clothes too clean, as if worn for the first time. The farmer spoke to me politely, indicating the cottage. 'Are your parents at home?'

'They don't live here,' I said. 'It's my grandparents'.'

'Ah.' He nodded. 'Of course. I wonder if I might speak to them?'

'They're not in.'

'No.' he said. 'I see.' He sniffed at the air, looked down at my jeans. 'Pigkeepers, I take it.'

'Yes.'

His eyes surveyed the garden behind me, the other man watching him. Satisfied, he nodded again, and said with a smile, 'Do I know you? I feel we've met before.'

I said, 'Are you going to buy this land?'

The younger man tugged at his nose and looked down at his feet. He was smiling. For a moment the farmer considered, narrowing his eyes, then suddenly laughed. He said, 'That deed is already done, my friend. A *fait accompli*.' He waited to see my response, and I nodded, shifted my weight to one leg. I shrugged, as if unconcerned. Glancing to the other man he said, 'Well, I must get on, but I expect we'll

meet again. Do mention to your grandparents that I called.'
I gave no reply and he smiled again. 'Cheerio then.' And
both men turned together, the farmer raising a hand as they
left me.

Indoors I stood at the kitchen table and read through my
letter to Surinder. I leaned an elbow on the table and
picked up the pencil. A minute passed, and more, and very
slowly, watching the words from a distance, I wrote, *I love
you*. Then I looked again, and carefully I tore the page
from the pad, slowly folded it into my fist. I dropped it in
the litter bin and went upstairs to the bedroom.

TWENTY-NINE

A S SURINDER came down the pathway I stood in
the half-light of the downstairs bedroom and
watched through the curtains. She was wearing her anorak,
a yellow T-shirt beneath it. Her hair blew loose on her
shoulders and she appeared self-conscious, walked with
exaggerated slowness. Her fingertips trailed through the
leaves of the hedge. She glanced at me once, then up to the
roof and across at the vegetables. I dragged the curtains
together and drew the bedclothes over the pillows. When
she entered the kitchen I was filling a kettle. 'Been sleeping?'
she said.

I shrugged.

'Your hair's all on end.' I smoothed a hand on my head,
and she added, 'Agnes looked pretty dopey as well.'

'She's dopey all the time,' I told her. 'She's sick.'

Surinder nodded and pulled out a chair from the table. I said, 'So where've you been all week?'

'Library.' As she sat down she read aloud from my notebook, 'Back soon. Grandad's ill.' Her face registered no shock or worry, and she said, 'You were expecting me then?'

'Yes,' I said lightly, 'he's feeling a lot better now, thank you.'

'Sorry.' She inclined her head until I faced her, then softly repeated, 'I'm sorry.'

I concentrated my gaze on a dent in the kettle. As the water started to boil the kettle shook on the hob. I said, 'Did you read anything interesting?'

'A few things. Some of it was interesting. What about you?'

'I opened Gran's mail.'

'And?'

'It was all bills and stuff. Boring. I couldn't be bothered reading it.'

There was a long silence. After some minutes Surinder sighed deeply, drummed her fingernails on the tabletop. Suddenly she stood and with her hands in her pockets she walked around the kitchen, looking at the plates and cups in the sink, Gran's raincoat on the back of the door, the old calendar over the cooker. She went through to the conservatory, but there was nothing she had not already seen. I followed her into the back room of the cottage with two mugs of tea. She stared at the cricket on the television. It glowed bright green in the gloom and when I switched on the light I saw that the clock had stopped. 'What's the time?' I said. She showed me her watch, a cheap plastic bracelet. 'Where'd you get that?'

'The shop.' She posed with her arms raised to each side, curtsying. 'Good, no?'

'No.' I picked up the photograph of my grandparents on their honeymoon, slipped it into my pocket. Then I wound the clock and set it back on the mantelpiece, ran my finger along the tiles. 'Everywhere needs dusting in here. It's miserable.'

'You're the one who's miserable.'

I showed her my teeth, a stiff smile. 'Okay?'

'Better.'

'Shall we go upstairs?'

She blew in her cup, nodding as I walked past her.

A strong draught descended the staircase. For a moment we were lit by the light of the front bedroom, then the door above us slammed shut. The sudden dark was familiar but my legs felt heavy, as if I was pulling Surinder behind me. I stumbled near the top step, splashed my tea on the wall. When I glanced back she seemed a long way below. I held the door until she reached me, felt her warmth as she ducked under my arm. Her hair brushed my face. I went and sat on the mattress.

Surinder remained standing a while longer. She looked around at this room also, at the bare stained walls and the ceiling. The bedclothes trailed on the floorboards, twisted and grubby. I touched the sheet which covered the mattress. 'Are you going to sit down at least?' I said. But she crossed to the window and fastened it, shivering slightly. The leaves had been rustling outside and a breeze was beginning to blow. Now it was quiet. She peered down at the garden as if looking for something, finally came and sat at my side. She cupped her mug under her chin and drew up her knees. Her shoulder touched mine. I said, 'Why don't you take off your anorak?'

'I'm not staying long,' she told me. 'I want to get back.'

'So why did you come out here?'

'Just thought I would, see how you were.'

'Thanks.' There was a packet of cigarettes on the floor. I said, 'Do you want a fag?'

She shook her head, made herself smile. 'Giving up,' she whispered.

I hesitated, holding the packet unopened. It made a nice shape in my hand, a nice weight, and I turned it over, pushed the top back with my thumb. The spongy ends of the filters were white and clean, the tobacco sweet-smelling. I drew out a cigarette. 'Me too,' I said, 'after this one.' We watched as the cigarette smouldered. The burning tip spiralled backwards, crackling and popping, turning the paper to ash. 'Can you hear it?' I whispered. 'Listen.'

Surinder looked at me and said, 'Is your grandad very ill?'

'He's just old,' I said, inhaling. 'He misses Gran. He had this fall on Monday, he fell out of bed and lay there ages waiting for someone to come. That's how he caught cold. He says he went to sleep on the floor and had a dream about Gran, but he can't remember what she said. He keeps trying to remember and he gets all frustrated. He really hates it when he can't remember stuff.'

'Did you tell him about the pig?'

'No, he'd just get upset.' I sighed. 'It was Gran who knew about things like this, practical things.'

Surinder waited. She said, 'He'd be sorry if he saw the garden now, wouldn't he?'

I nodded. The weeds from the neighbouring plots had begun to spread through Gran's roses, and the hedges were wild, sprouting new shoots, in places as tall as the apple trees. Once there had been clear borders, a lawn which stopped where the flowerbeds began, neatly trimmed edges. On sunny days I had sat in a deckchair beside Grandad, listening to his voice and watching my grandmother. Always there was the noise of the steelworks, lorries rattling along the main road. Now the lawn was no different from the land which surrounded it. In the allotment the leaves of the vegetables were being eaten by insects and caterpillars. The trees were dropping their fruit on to nettles. I said, 'Shall we go out to the country? We could pick up some straw. Nick some from a field or something.'

Surinder said, 'Not now, Danny.'

Her voice was very quiet, and I said, 'The pig really smells, doesn't she?'

'It's not Agnes,' she sighed, 'it's the rubbish tip. It stinks.' I flattened the cigarette beneath my heel, exhaled the smoke through my nose. 'It's foul, Danny. It's like the smell at the back of Dad's shop, where the bins are. It hits you as soon as you come up the drive.'

'They'll probably fill it in soon anyway,' I said. 'Or empty it or something. My brother reckons they're going to build a model railway. They'll have steam trains chugging round the quarries all day.' I fell back on the mattress and drew the bedclothes over my legs. 'Maybe they'll turn this place into a museum. They could make waxworks of Gran and Grandad, sell pottery pigs and stuff. They might offer us jobs.' Surinder drank from her mug, placed it next to mine on the boards. She wasn't smiling. I said flatly, 'That guy's been round. The farmer we met in the country, the one with the Land-Rover.'

'Here?' She looked puzzled, annoyed. 'Why?'

'Just nosing about.' I pulled the bedding to my chin. 'He says he's bought the land. He was wandering all over, sizing everything up.'

'But that's disgusting!' She lay on her belly beside me. 'He's really horrible, Danny. What does he want it for?'

'Don't know. But he's coming back to talk to Gran about it.' Surinder narrowed her eyes. I lifted one edge of the eiderdown. 'Do you want to get in?' For a moment she seemed reluctant, but then eased herself to the middle of the mattress and allowed me to enclose her. She crossed her arms on her chest, her hands on her shoulder blades. I laid my hand in the curve of her waist. With my forehead touching hers I murmured, 'I was writing you a letter, you know, before he turned up.'

'What about?'

'Us.' I shrugged. 'The cottage and the pig and everything.'

'Is that us?'

'Suppose not.' With an effort I kicked off my shoes, heard them clump on the floorboards.

'What are you doing?'

'Nothing.' I kissed her.

'Tell me what you wrote.'

'Well, I mentioned about Grandad, how he was sick and everything.'

'That's not about us.'

'No. But then I said about leaving school.' Reaching between us I tugged her belt through its buckle, unfastened the top stud on her jeans. 'I said I was going to move out here permanently, maybe get a job and try and breed some pigs, do it all properly.'

Her anorak rustled. She clamped her hand on my wrist, over my bangle. 'Just you?'

'Would you have come too?'

She sucked in her bottom lip, shook her head gently.

'I thought not,' I said.

Surinder watched my face as I kissed her, her mouth unresponding, half-smiling. 'What else?' she said.

'Nothing much . . .' I eased myself from her grip and found the next stud, pushed it back through the eyelet. 'It doesn't really matter now,' I said. I pulled one side of her jeans to her hips, and she lifted herself a fraction to help me, again crossed her arms on her chest. Her face was close to mine, too near to focus, and when I lowered one eyelid she copied me, as if in a mirror.

'It does matter,' she insisted.

'It wasn't much of a letter anyway,' I said. 'Half a page.'

'Danny!'

'Surinder?'

I smiled as I drew the bedclothes over my head. In the warmth of her closeness I could smell the smoke on my fingers, damp and age in the blankets, a mustiness from childhood. I eased her jeans to her ankles, pressed my nose to her skin. Her scent was familiar; it was clammy and sweet and she left it sometimes on my hands, in my clothes. I breathed deeply. I wanted to remember.

When I surfaced she hooked her arms around me. 'It sounds really boring,' she said. 'Why did you write it?'

'I didn't think I'd see you again.'

She drew my top lip between her teeth, gently bit me. 'So what are we going to do?'

'Run away and get married?'

Surinder smiled but her smile quickly faded. With her hands loosely clasped on my neck she examined my face, pressed her nose against mine. A film of tears blurred her eyes. Quietly she said, 'Are you going to take off your trousers, Danny?'

The light faded as the clouds darkened over the quarries. The cries of the gulls were carried away on the wind. I unstrapped my belt and arched my back on the mattress, tugged down my jeans and my underpants. Surinder curled herself beneath the eiderdown, her face pillowed in her hair, watching as I folded my jeans, carefully laid them on the floor at my side. She did not remove her anorak and I did not unbutton my shirt. I rolled onto my side, pressed my leg between hers. 'Tell me what else you wrote,' she said.

'Nothing,' I said. I took a long breath. 'Just that I wanted you to have Gran's ring.'

'Again?'

'As a souvenir.'

'To remember you by?'

'For always and always.'

Surinder raised herself on her elbows and knees, crouching above me. 'Okay,' she said. 'If you want me to have it.' She allowed her hair to tickle my face. I grinned as I blew it away.

'It's in my jeans.'

'Later,' she said.

As she guided me inside her I touched her hand gently with mine. Slowly she eased forwards and back. The open flaps of her anorak hung on each side of me, smelling of plastic and perfume, her sweat from the garden. I buried my face in her shoulder and held her against me. She cradled my head in her hands. I murmured her name, and closing my eyes I felt only her softness, and then, as our breathing became heavier, a moist, distant sensation, which was over in seconds. It was the last time. Surinder continued to move against me. And when I found her face to kiss her I saw that she was crying. I dragged a blanket from our legs and draped us beneath it. In the darkness we lay without moving.

Finally she whispered, 'Can I have that fag now?'

'Do you want to share one?'

'Okay.' She sat upright, wiped her eyes in her T-shirt. I struck a match to the cigarette, and she said, 'How's your pregnant sister now, Danny?'

'Still pregnant.' I shrugged. 'She's keeping out of the way. Why?'

Surinder accepted the cigarette. 'Just wondering.'

'Right.' And I nodded, waiting for my turn to smoke. 'How's your pregnant sister-in-law?' I asked.

'Gone home now.'

I nodded.

'Back to the shop. They're going to open it again.'

'Right.'

There was a long pause. Surinder drew deeply on the cigarette, turned away as she exhaled. She coughed, spluttering on the smoke, and I realized then that she was sobbing. Her shoulders heaved and I wrapped my arms around her, tried to still her shaking. The cigarette dropped from her fingers to the floorboards. 'What's up?' I murmured, but she didn't reply. I touched her face, felt her tears on my hand. 'Don't cry,' I whispered.

The voices downstairs were muffled, arrived as if from a distance. I lifted my head a little to hear them, and recognized my brother. He was talking to Dad. They were in my grandparents' bedroom beneath us. For some moments I did not move, felt no urgency or fear. I laid my cheek on Surinder's, listened as they walked through to the back room. Then a hand fumbled the latch at the foot of the staircase. 'Fuck's sake,' I sighed, and reached for my jeans. Surinder looked at me, her eyes swollen, uncomprehending. I flapped at the air in front of my face, a grey haze of cigarette smoke, and scrambled to gather her clothes. 'Quick,' I said.

Her face was calm and resigned and she did not hurry. As she pushed her legs into her jeans she stared at the floor, as if lost in thought. She was barefoot when Richard arrived at the top of the stairs, still fastening the studs on her flies. She held his gaze until he began to redden, then crouched at the mattress and pulled her knickers from under the bedclothes. She bunched them into her anorak pocket and stepped into her sandals, facing me without expression. The mattress was between us. I stepped towards her, felt as if I was crossing the length of the room.

Richard said, 'You disgusting little toerag, Danny.' His voice was harsh and unsteady and he called down to my father, 'He's up here!' Then glanced at Surinder, his colour deepening, and added, 'With a girl!' I saw the top of my father's head as he mounted the stairs, and took Surinder's hand in mine. It was cold. I realized I was sweating. Richard said, 'She's a paki, Dad. His girlfriend's a fucking Pakistani.'

THIRTY

THE FOLLOWING morning I woke later than usual, and lay for much longer, as if weighted to the bed, unable to move. From outside in the square I heard my brother laughing, a sudden shout and the snap of a beer can. The front door was open. Several voices competed at once, suddenly louder as they came into our hallway. I heard Richard trying to calm them, and the front door closing. There was a brief pause, a low murmur, and the laughter began again in our living room. Rain spattered my window, coming louder when the wind blew, gently subsiding. The light was grainy and blue. Objects appeared indistinct and seemed to move when I looked at them. I reached backwards and pulled on the light cord, stared up at the ceiling.

In my dream I had been trying to inflate the front tyre of

my grandmother's bicycle. I was kneeling in Surinder's
front garden and seated on the wall at my side were Spider
and Stan, sharing one of my cigarettes. They were waiting
for our new neighbours to arrive and although it was
daytime the air around us had the texture of darkness.
Surinder's bedroom window was brightly illuminated.
'She'll be at the library,' Stan told me. But I pretended not
to have heard him. I continued to pump air into the tyre,
explaining about the design of the valve, the pounds per
inch pressure in the pump and the anatomy of my arm. I
spoke in a low, informative tone, but their faces showed no
interest. The tyre remained flat.

When Surinder appeared at my side she was wearing a
black maternity smock that belonged to my sister. I noticed
that her breasts were much larger and wondered how much
air they contained. She stared contemptuously at Spider
and Stan, and I whispered into her ear, 'I gave them the
fag, Surinder. I thought they'd go away but I just can't
seem to get rid of them.'

She screwed the cap on a fountain pen, and said coolly,
'How's Agnes?'

I shrugged. 'It's hopeless, I tried to get some air into her
this morning, but it's this pump, it's broken.'

'She doesn't mind about her ring then?'

Surinder showed me her profile and I saw that she was
wearing a gold hoop through one nostril. It glinted in the
darkness. As I looked closely, trying to decide if it was
Gran's, I heard laughter behind me and spun around to
face Spider and Stan. They were dismantling the bicycle,
using hammers to break up the parts. Stan held the front
wheel to the side of his nose. Spider looped the chain
around his wrist as a bracelet. It was the hammering which
had woken me.

The front door opened and slammed shut. I quickly rose

and peered round my curtains. I did not recognize Richard's friends. One of them paused at the door to the bungalow unit and looked into the recess. He was laughing as he hurried after the others. He put his hand on Richard's shoulder and they turned towards the centre of the estate, walking briskly, their footsteps resounding in the passage-way. I let the curtains fall and picked up my clock. It was after eleven and I supposed they would be going to the pub. I had not realized it was so late.

In the kitchen I pulled on my trainers and left the kettle to boil. Outside the rain had eased to a drizzle and the air smelled of damp concrete. Large patches of wet darkened the fronts of the houses. Puddles had formed where the paving slabs were uneven. As I approached the door of the bungalow I folded my arms on my chest and hunched up my shoulders. The water which was gathering at the base of the doorstep was pink. I remembered the slabs of meat that Ted had brought to my grandparents' cottage, how they had stained their newspaper wrappings and seeped onto the kitchen table. I thought I knew what I would see. But I did not expect the piles of shit in the recess.

There was toilet tissue too, sodden blue strips torn from the roll in our house. The stench clutched at my throat and I held a hand to my mouth. I looked for a message, but the graffiti on the walls had been there for months. The pig's trotters were nailed to the door. They were inverted and scraggy and the flesh was drained of colour. The few remaining hairs were grey. Holding my breath I tried to remove them but they would not come and I thought I was going to be sick. I stepped backwards and glimpsed my brother's overcoat in our hallway. I ran towards it. It was hanging from a peg at the foot of the stairs, where he had left it after Gran's funeral. I remembered how he had appeared at the back of the chapel, and then amongst the wreaths outside, pale and sweating in the sunshine. He had made a joke about bacon prices, gripped my arm when I tried to walk past him. As I pulled down the coat I heard the toilet flushing above me. My father appeared on the landing. For some moments he stared without speaking, then he shook his head and passed into the bedroom. I emptied his toolbox onto the carpet and searched for his pliers.

In the recess I laid Richard's coat over the shit and tramped it down flat. The foul smell remained, but as I worked the nails from the door I kept my teeth clenched, tried not to inhale. When finally the trotters came free they tore two splinters from the wood, exposed the yellow timber beneath the red paintwork. The old woman on the other side of the square was watching around her net curtains. I took my brother's coat by the collar and dragged it from the recess, trailed it to the porch of Pete's house in the corner. I left it on his doorstep and returned to our house with the trotters, still pierced by their nails. In the kitchen the kettle was boiling over. The water spilled onto the floor and sent a cloud of vapour to the ceiling. I pulled on my jacket and left the house by the back door.

Richard was not in the pub. The lounge was dim-lit and empty, the beer mats neatly arranged on the tables. There were no cigarette butts in the ashtrays and no empty glasses. A video games console flashed orange and green in one corner, spluttered to life as I went into the bar. A few men looked up without curiosity. I scanned their faces and turned for the toilets, a sudden thick smell of urine. A man's voice shouted, 'Out of there!' but I let the doors swing behind me and kicked open each of the cubicles. When I came out again the landlord was lifting the bar hatch. His belly was large and he had to raise himself onto his toes to squeeze through. 'Looking for my brother,' I said. 'He's not here.' And I pushed over a chair as I left.

I cycled in a damp and gusting wind with the trotters in my basket. Ahead of me the tarmac and sky were grey, trees bending with the wind on either side of the road. Dark clouds scudded over my head from the quarries. The windscreens of the cars that approached me were spattered with rain, the drizzle dully illuminated in their headlamps. The bicycle couldn't be made to accelerate and my limbs soon tired of its weight. I dropped my head and pushed wearily on each pedal, watching the road as it passed under the wheels.

When I turned off the dual carriageway the cycle skidded in the damp gravel of the driveway. Ahead of me I could see the red transit van, its rear doors half open. It was parked at the gate to Gran's garden. I slid from my saddle and ran up the hill, dragging the rattling bicycle beside me. Richard's friend Craig was in the allotment, leaning against the sty wall. He looked up and watched me. He was chewing, and seemed to be waiting. I dropped the bike on the ground and took the trotters from the basket, approached the sty slowly, smelling the damp in the air, the stench of the tip. 'Alright, mate?' he said. 'What's up?'

I began to speak but my mouth was too tight. I held up the trotters, seeing him dimly. 'What's this?' he said, smiling, and I knew from his voice that he did not know. I shook my head. In the sty the pig was lying on her side, her eyes glassy and lifeless, seeming to watch us. He said, 'It's just a chill probably, she's getting old. I'd get a vet out to her this afternoon. She might come round yet.' The pig's abdomen filled, her snout narrowed. I counted her trotters, clenched my teeth against the relief that rose through me. 'Really you ought to get some straw for her,' he continued. 'That grass in there is damp. Mouldy.' I glanced at him then, and noticed the gold ring in his ear. I thought of Surinder, the first time she had stood with me at the sty, how she had appeared in my dream that morning. She would not come again to the cottage, nor to see Grandad. And I knew now that I would not be returning to school. I wiped my eyes on my sleeve, still gripping the trotters, and heard Craig ask me, 'What's with the hocks anyway?'

'Nothing.' I threw them out of the garden, towards his red van. I was smiling. 'Doesn't matter.' The pig was watching me. I leant on the wall and whistled, but she did not respond.

Craig said, 'There's some smell off that tip now.'

'Yeah.'

'I hear Richard's got a job across the way. Fucking waste of time that.'

Remembering, I said, 'He got laid off. The owners have changed.'

He nodded. 'Figures,' he said, and pointed to the pig as he turned for the van. 'Phone for a vet anyway. She'll maybe pull round.'

But my grandparents did not have a phone. Gran did not like them. As the van reversed down the driveway I went indoors for her raincoat. The quilting inside smelled now of Surinder. I caught her perfume as I took it down from the hook. It was in the sleeves too, in the collar, and for the rest of the afternoon I breathed her scent as I cleared the garden. I tore up the pegs and lines which had marked my grandmother's vegetables, collected the sticks on which she'd attached her seed packets, the colours now faded and the names barely legible. I bundled them into the wheelbarrow. Here and there she had planted a bamboo cane, a piece of tin toil attached to the end. They were supposed to scare off the birds but they had not worked since my childhood. I tugged them from the soil and tossed them into the barrow, began to dismantle her bean trellis. Finally I forked up the vegetables. For three hours I pushed one load after another to the corner of the garden, tipping the remains of the allotment into the railway cutting. Damp soil caked my trainers and the rain dripped from my face. I stopped to gaze around me, allowed the fork to tip backwards into a pile of dung. Gran's basket still stood in the soil, but there was no garden now, nothing else that remained of her. Soon the cottage would also come down. I wondered if the tip would expand, become official, approved by the Council. Perhaps *LeisureLand* would start again, or new factories come. On the far side of the tip the *LeisureLand* hoarding was streaked with bird droppings and the paint was flaking, showing patches of grey wood. There was no activity near the quarries.

The pig did not stir as I worked, and although I looked in on her regularly she showed no interest in me. Indoors her swill pot was mouldy and cold. I dropped the pot in the sink and pulled open the drawer which contained my grandmother's knives. I selected the largest and touched the blade with the pad of my forefinger. It might have been blunt or sharp, I didn't know how to tell. I made a nick in the table between the cigarette burns. The cut was shallow and broad and I took the knife to the grinding wheel in the conservatory. I turned the handle rapidly and when the wheel was revolving faster than my arm I pressed the blade to the stone.

I sat with the pig in her shelter and watched the tired pulse of the vein in her neck. She glanced at me when I moved, but mostly stared into space. Her snout was warm and dry. She did not flinch when I held the blade to her throat. The rain fell heavily, splashing in the puddles on the floor of the sty. I remembered my grandfather's description of the slaughterhouse, wondered if I should stun her beforehand, bring a hammer from the conservatory. I pictured a blow to her skull, and laid the knife on the ground at my side. I stood outside in the rain and encouraged her to stand, calling as my grandmother had done. With an effort the pig rose to her feet, standing unsteadily, legs trembling, and I shouted, 'Yes! Good girl!' But she turned and went deeper into her shelter. She flopped onto her side on the grass, her legs almost straight, still trembling. I crawled in beside her and sat with my back to the rear of the shelter, facing out to her pen and the run to the gate, the wall where our faces would have appeared to her. The rain fell vertically, drummed on the roof, the floor of the sty. I lifted her head onto my lap.

When I went indoors it was turning dark and the rain was still pouring. I tried the light switch. There was no power. In the conservatory I felt the chill and damp of the hours spent outside, and the cold which had always been here. I found the coal hole by its smell, and reached out a hand for the scuttle. When I was smaller I had hidden in here. Later Gran had sent me to fetch coal. I could find my way without seeing, but when I stooped to fill the scuttle now I felt suddenly afraid and lifted my head. I stared into the blackness, willing an image to form, familiar shapes in their usual places. The heavy damp in my jeans chafed at my skin. I shivered, and felt my legs and arms continue to shake. My teeth were chattering. I left the scuttle where it lay and made my way to the stairs.

In the gloom of the back bedroom I stood quite still until my eyes became accustomed to the darkness. What light there was shimmered in the wire of the bed base. I sat on the edge of the frame, flexing my hands on the wires. The frame rocked into the wall. I gazed at my reflection in the wardrobe mirror, the wallpaper behind me, black sky through the window where the steelworks had been. Somewhere on top of the wardrobe there was a paraffin heater. I stood on a cabinet and fumbled amongst the boxes and dust until I found it. An animal scurried across the ceiling, a mouse perhaps, a bird in the attic. I took off my wet jeans and threw them onto the bed frame, walked through to the front room.

On the bare boards I could see some flower petals, white and shrivelled in the moonlight. One of Surinder's books lay face down and open beside the mattress. She had left a hairbrush. There was the box of matches, the cigarette stubs we had smoked yesterday. Richard had taken the rest of the pack. I struck a match to the heater and went across to the window, the blue flame flickering in the glass, burning behind me, a low roar as I stared out at the garden. The wind came softly from a distance, muffled, and then it was quiet. Rain streamed down the window.

I could smell the blood which had seeped through my jeans, feel it drying on my legs. The pig still lay in her shelter, the knife at her side in the grass. In the morning I would dig a hole for her, away from the compost, the rats' nest, amongst the trees perhaps. I looked down, forced Surinder's bangle over my hand. It tore the skin as it went over my thumb, and I swore, clenching my teeth. I held it to my eye, as she had done, stared into my reflection in the glass, faint in the dim light. Its proper name began with a k. K for *kara*. She had taught me other words too, and I tried to recall them, tried to remember her voice in this room, all she had said to me, all we had done. I did not want to forget.

READ MORE IN PENGUIN

In every corner of the world, on every subject under the sun, Penguin represents quality and variety – the very best in publishing today.

For complete information about books available from Penguin – including Puffins, Penguin Classics and Arkana – and how to order them, write to us at the appropriate address below. Please note that for copyright reasons the selection of books varies from country to country.

In the United Kingdom: Please write to *Dept. JC, Penguin Books Ltd, FREEPOST, West Drayton, Middlesex UB7 OBR.*

If you have any difficulty in obtaining a title, please send your order with the correct money, plus ten per cent for postage and packaging, to *PO Box No. 11, West Drayton, Middlesex UB7 OBR*

In the United States: Please write to *Consumer Sales, Penguin USA, P.O. Box 999, Dept. 17109, Bergenfield, New Jersey 07621-0120.* VISA and MasterCard holders call 1-800-253-6476 to order all Penguin titles

In Canada: Please write to *Penguin Books Canada Ltd, 10 Alcorn Avenue, Suite 300, Toronto, Ontario M4V 3B2*

In Australia: Please write to *Penguin Books Australia Ltd, P.O. Box 257, Ringwood, Victoria 3134*

In New Zealand: Please write to *Penguin Books (NZ) Ltd, Private Bag 102902, North Shore Mail Centre, Auckland 10*

In India: Please write to *Penguin Books India Pvt Ltd, 706 Eros Apartments, 56 Nehru Place, New Delhi 110 019*

In the Netherlands: Please write to *Penguin Books Netherlands bv, Postbus 3507, NL-1001 AH Amsterdam*

In Germany: Please write to *Penguin Books Deutschland GmbH, Metzlerstrasse 26, 60594 Frankfurt am Main*

In Spain: Please write to *Penguin Books S. A., Bravo Murillo 19, 1° B, 28015 Madrid*

In Italy: Please write to *Penguin Italia s.r.l., Via Felice Casati 20, I–20124 Milano*

In France: Please write to *Penguin France S. A., 17 rue Lejeune, F–31000 Toulouse*

In Japan: Please write to *Penguin Books Japan, Ishikiribashi Building, 2–5–4, Suido, Bunkyo-ku, Tokyo 112*

In Greece: Please write to *Penguin Hellas Ltd, Dimocritou 3, GR–106 71 Athens*

In South Africa: Please write to *Longman Penguin Southern Africa (Pty) Ltd, Private Bag X08, Bertsham 2013*

READ MORE IN PENGUIN

A CHOICE OF FICTION

Sacred Hunger Barry Unsworth

'Unsworth's theme is human rivalry; his subject is the slave trade of the mid-eighteenth century . . . *Sacred Hunger* is a tremendous performance. Not the least of its achievements is the sense of blood, guts and hurricanes existing side by side with an imaginatively realized interior life' – *Sunday Times*

The Vicar of Sorrows A. N. Wilson

'Hard to resist . . . scoring at least three unequivocal triumphs – as a bleakly funny portrait of male mid-life breakdown, as a serious piece of anti-theology and as a satire on Anglicanism' – *Daily Telegraph*

Mayday Jonathan Lynn

'A very funny, insightful and intelligent book and a taut thriller which will keep you turning the pages right to the surprising end' – Eric Idle. '*Mayday* is not a cry for help – it is a yelp for joy. Lynn's movie moguls, mysteries and mishaps leap straight off the page' – Maureen Lipman

Cal Bernard Mac Laverty

Springing out of the fear and violence of Ulster, Cal is a haunting love story in a land where tenderness and innocence can only flicker briefly in the dark. 'A gripping political thriller and a formidable fictional triumph' – *Observer*

Bridie and Finn Harry Cauley

Bridie and Finn are like chalk and cheese. She's motherless and loquacious. He's the quiet type, with a crooked leg from birth. And they become the best of friends. True to the unpredictable twists and turns of life, *Bridie and Finn* creates a hugely memorable mosaic of human relationships.